Spreading his arms like an eagle,
Stanley went crashing
through the audience as he charged
toward the food.

Kids scrambled frantically to get out of his path.

When he reached the first table, he squatted down in front of a plate of hot dog cupcakes and opened his mouth wide. The cupcakes were gone in twenty seconds.

Stanley moved on to the next plate, which was heaped with raw mushrooms stuffed with gumdrops. In a few more seconds that plate, too, was empty.

Everyone was staring at him with their hands over their mouths. Wendell Rice looked ready to pop.

In fewer than five minutes all four tables were empty.

I squinted through the window to see Elayne Munter frantically adding up numbers on her notepad. After a few more seconds she shouted, "Listen, guys! Sam Moore just ate forty-five platefuls of gross food! So let's give Sam a big, big—"

Burp. A big, big burp. It came from Stanley.

And it practically blew everyone across the playground.

STINKY STANLEY
STINKS AGAIN ™

ANN HODGMAN

Illustrated by
John Emil Cymerman

A GLC BOOK

A
MINSTREL®
BOOK

PUBLISHED BY POCKET BOOKS

New York   London   Toronto   Sydney   Tokyo   Singapore

For Charlie, Jamie, and Evan

A MINSTREL PAPERBACK *ORIGINAL*

A Minstrel Book published by
POCKET BOOKS, a division of Simon & Schuster Inc.
1230 Avenue of the Americas, New York, NY 10020

Special thanks to Pat MacDonald and Elise Howard

Developed by Byron Preiss and Daniel Weiss
Edited by Lisa Meltzer
Cover painting by Jeffrey Lindberg
Illustrations by John Emil Cymerman
Typesetting by Jackson Typesetting Company

ISBN: 0-671-78560-5

First Minstrel Books printing December 1993

10 9 8 7 6 5 4 3 2 1

Printed in the U.S.A.

CHAPTER ONE

Moving Day

"Stanley, will you please pass me the hammer?" I asked my almost-identical twin one afternoon after school. We were building a tree house together.

Stanley wiped his nose on the hammer and passed it to me. "Here am hammer, Sam," he told me proudly.

"Uh—thanks," I said, taking the hammer gingerly. A slimy green booger was oozing down the handle. "But, Stanley, it's not a good idea to get boogers on tools."

"Yeah," chimed in my Uncle Zachary, who was helping us with the tree house. "The tools might rust."

I wiped the hammer with an old rag. "Could I have a nail, too?" I asked Stanley.

He stuck his thumb into his mouth, bit off a strip of thumbnail with his teeth, and spit it wetly into my hand. "Here am nail," he said.

"Sorry," I said. "That's not what I meant." I wiped my hand on my jeans and pointed at the box behind him. *"Those* are the nails I'm using."

This time Stanley got it right. "Thank you," I said.

"UUUUUuuuhhhhhhUUUUUUUhhhhhRRR-RRRrrrrrrrrrp!" burped Stanley in reply. Then he scratched his armpits like a chimpanzee and blew his nose into his fingers.

It was probably a good thing Uncle Zach and I were building a tree house for Stanley. Someone like my twin just can't live in a regular house with regular people. Stanley has his own way of doing things. He needs his own space—or maybe what I mean is, normal people need space from *him.*

Let me go back a little and explain. Stanley isn't my "birth twin," or whatever you'd call it. He's really kind of a . . . mistake. He was created, not born.

One morning a few weeks ago, Uncle Zachary—who's a scientist—handed me a blob of protoplasm he had generated in his lab. (The lab is in the basement of my house, which Uncle Zach rents from my parents.) I dropped the protoplasm—you would have done the same thing, believe me—and it had to be thrown away. But later that day lightning struck the garbage can when I was standing right next to it, and the next thing I knew, a guy who looked exactly like me was crawling out and hugging me and breathing his stinky breath all over me. I named him Stanley.

My parents don't know about Stanley, of course. (Would you tell *your* parents about something like him?) For the first week of his life he lived in Uncle Zachary's lab. Uncle Zach and I knew that wouldn't work forever, though, so we decided to make him a tree house. The tree we chose was in the little strip of woods behind my backyard. We figured my parents would never find it there. They don't like to go out into nature much.

I glanced up at Uncle Zach, who was trying to hang the tree house door. Stanley and I were supposed to be helping him, but it was really the other way around. My uncle is a scientific genius, but he's not much of a carpenter.

"I have a feeling I'm putting this door on backward, Sam," he grunted as he wrestled with the door.

"Oh, well. It won't make any difference to Stanley," I said, consoling him. "He'll probably never close the door anyway."

"Squirrels come in see me!" Stanley shouted excitedly. "Squirrels! Mouses! Birds! Skunks!"

Uncle Zachary looked at him. "You want *skunks* up here?" he asked.

"Skunks nice," Stanley explained. "They pretty!"

I grinned. "Everyone's got his own style, Uncle Zach. Some people like fancy furniture. *You* like a messy lab filled with weird experiments. Stanley likes skunks."

"I keep forgetting what an original thinker he is," said Uncle Zachary, beaming with pride. "Skunks it is, then! Nothing's too good for my—uh—nephew? Or whatever."

That's a good question. Stanley isn't exactly my brother, so he's not really Uncle Zach's nephew. I don't even know if he counts as a person. But he is identical to me, at least when you clean him up. This doesn't happen often, because it takes hours and only lasts for minutes.

"Where Mawyahnee?" Stanley suddenly asked now.

That's his name for Marjorie Cass. Marjorie's a friend of mine who lives down the street. She's a fifth-grader, like me, but we're not in the same class at school. Stanley loves her. He drools over her—literally.

"Marjorie had to do something with her mother," I explained. "She'll be over tomorrow to see your new house."

I glanced around. It was going to be a nice tree house. But we had tried to camouflage it as much as possible. The roof had branches nailed on top, and the windows were hidden behind bark shutters. We had also given Stanley a rope ladder that he could pull up after himself and hide—if he remembered to pull it up. I wasn't sure he would.

Inside, we had decorated according to Stanley's

tastes. We'd built a bed into the wall and a little bookcase with all the kinds of books my twin liked best. *A Field Guide to Worms* was his favorite at the moment. Second-favorite was an old science book of Uncle Zachary's called *Introduction to Pus*. Stanley couldn't read yet—there hadn't been time to teach him so far—but he loved to look at the pictures.

Stanley had added his own little touches by smearing earwax everywhere.

Yes, the new tree house was going to be the perfect spot for him. I just hoped he would be happy there and not wander around too much. When Stanley starts wandering, things get a little out of control.

"Hey, Sam!" Marjorie called from behind me. "Wait up!"

It was the next day. I was walking across the playground toward the school buses. School had just let out, and I was eager to get home and see how Stanley's first day in his tree house had gone.

I was also eager to get home to start thinking about ways to get some money. My school had just decided to have a fund-raising contest to buy trees for the school grounds—not that trees would make coming to school any more fun.

Each grade would compete against the others. The grade that raised the most money would get to pick out a prize. Of course the "prize" had to be something the whole school could use. (There's always a catch.) The teachers were going in the direction of a new set of encyclopedias for the media center. The kids were going in the direction of a wave machine in the swimming pool, so we could surf.

"Well?" Marjorie panted when she caught up to me. "Have you thought of anything yet?"

I couldn't help laughing. "Marjorie, they just announced the contest ten minutes ago! Give me a chance!"

"We could sell something, maybe," Marjorie suggested. "Wrapping paper or something like that."

"The sixth-graders sold wrapping paper last year," I reminded her. "Remember how they ran out of everything except that tissue paper with fire engines on it?"

"How about candy, then?"

"Seems too babyish," I said. "We'd better—"

"Hello, Samuel. Hello, Marjorie," came a prissy voice from behind us.

Marjorie and I exchanged looks of disgust before we turned around. "Hello, Wendell," we said in unison.

Wendell Rice is just about my least favorite person in the world. He's the class genius. He flosses his teeth in the boys' room after lunch. He never uses nicknames and he's never late to school and he never does anything wrong—almost never, anyway. He's such a whiny, wimpy, show-offy goody-goody that even the teachers don't like him much.

Before Stanley came along, I wasn't friends with too many kids besides Wendell (and Marjorie, of course). My nerdy parents made it hard for me to live a normal life, and Wendell was just the kind of kid they liked me to spend time with. He and I used to—I'm embarrassed to admit this—study together at the library on Saturday mornings. Now I never do weird stuff like that.

Having Stanley around has changed my life—a lot. I used to be totally under my parents' thumb. (Thumbs? Well, whatever.) They made me dress like a miniature grown-up—complete with white shirts with pocket protectors—and checked my tissues to see if I had a cold and did lots of other horrible, picky stuff. And I just let them do it. (Dad kept telling me when I grew up I could dress the way *I* wanted.)

But Stanley is so much *not* the kind of person who acts like a miniature grown-up that he loosened me up a lot. (Anyway, being grown up is just too far away to wait for.) I'm very grateful to Stanley. Now I get away with a lot more than I used to.

For instance, I do a quick change out of my Mom-and-Dad-picked clothes into regular jeans and stuff every morning before I leave for school. My parents leave the house before I do—they're accountants, and they have an accounting business called Moore & Moore. Uncle Zach is in the lab by the time I leave, but he doesn't notice what I wear. Things like that aren't important to him.

I also save Mom's weird leftovers for Stanley and buy normal food for myself, like cheeseburgers and potato chips. (My parents give me a decent allowance, at least, so I can buy myself the things I need from time to time.) Also, I have lots more friends now.

Anyway, back to Wendell. Ever since I accidentally got him into trouble in a food fight in our school cafeteria, Wendell has pretty much hated me. Which is kind of a relief, of course. But I guess that that afternoon he felt like talking to someone, and Marjorie and I happened to be the first victims he caught.

"I have a *superb* idea for a fund-raiser," he said importantly. "A science contest. Each fifth-grader will choose a topic and memorize as many scientific facts about it as he or she can. My topic will be the circulatory system of the squid, I think. Then we'll hold a contest in the auditorium to see who knows the most facts. We'll charge admission, of course. It will raise money *and* be educational! What do you two think?"

"Sounds terrible," said Marjorie bluntly.

"That's a nice attitude!" Wendell snapped. "I can see *you're* going to get a great education!"

I tried to be a little more diplomatic, hoping that would get rid of Wendell faster. "It sounds very interesting," I said carefully, "but I'm not sure how much money it would raise. Do you think people would pay to watch a contest like that—especially kids?"

Now Wendell became all sharp eyed and ruffled, like an angry hen. "Obviously I'm dealing with inferior minds here!" he said. "I don't know why I waste my time with people like you!"

"I don't, either," I whispered to Marjorie as we watched Wendell storm away.

"Oh, well," said Marjorie. "At least it will be easy to come up with an idea that's better than *his*."

We got onto our bus—as always, we sat at opposite ends. (It wasn't "cool" for boys and girls to sit together on the bus.) I knew Marjorie would be coming over to my house after school. Marjorie loves Stanley as much as he loves her. He's almost like a pet to her. One that's barely housebroken, of course.

Once, when Stanley still lived in Uncle Zachary's lab, he let all kinds of wild animals into the house while I was at school. So I was a little worried about what I'd find when I got to the tree house that afternoon. Uncle Zachary is in his lab during the day. He promised to keep an eye on Stanley when he was there. It still left Stanley alone a lot, though.

When Marjorie and I got to the tree house, I was relieved to see that Stanley hadn't actually invited any skunks in. Instead, he had found a bunch of slugs and snails and decorated the outside of the tree house with them.

"I guess that's his idea of a wreath," I said to Marjorie as I climbed the rope ladder toward the tree house. "Hi, Stanley!" I called. "The slugs look great!"

Stanley didn't answer. He had just spotted Marjorie coming up the ladder behind me. He threw himself out of the tree house, hit the ground, and then bounced back up to the tree house and swung from a branch. Stanley has some unusual powers, and bouncing was one he had just discovered. He spent a lot of time practicing it. He could also turn his ears inside out, but you don't want to hear about that.

Now, having finished his bouncing, Stanley flattened himself out to the thickness of a sheet of paper and slithered under the tree house door. (That's another little talent he has.) Then he opened the door with a flourish.

"Mawyahnee!" he whooped. "Hi! Hi! House worm

books bed nails hammer door Uncle Zachary!"

I guess he was trying to tell Marjorie the story of how we'd built the tree house.

"Hi, Stanley," Marjorie said warmly. "Hey, are you okay? Did you hurt yourself?"

Stanley nodded proudly. "Bounce! Bump nose! Fun!" he exclaimed. He sucked a booger down his throat and swallowed it with relish.

Marjorie and I both gulped. "I'm glad you're all right," Marjorie said weakly. She peered through the tree house's front window. "Wow! I—uh— like the way you've spread all that garbage around in here. Good job!"

Marjorie and I try to accept Stanley the way he is. It's not that we *like* him being so messy, but we don't want to be too critical, either. Besides, Stanley's not bad compared to my parents' super-neatness.

"Good job," Stanley echoed, nodding his head so furiously that dandruff sprayed into the air like snow from a snowblower. Then he plucked a snail off the front door and popped it into his mouth like a piece of popcorn.

"Don't!" I protested, wincing. The snail's shell made an awful crunching sound between Stanley's teeth. "Not live like that! I'll get you something from the kitchen—"

Suddenly I stopped. "The kitchen," I said slowly. "Stanley . . . the fund-raiser . . ."

"I hope Stanley's way of talking isn't catching," Marjorie said. "If it is, I'm getting out of here."

"No, no, it's not that," I said. "I just had an idea for how the fifth grade can raise money. It'll be a lot more fun than Wendell's science contest, too."

Then I turned to Stanley. "And *you* are going to be the star!"

CHAPTER TWO

Soft-Boiled Eggs with Sugar Lumps

"A gross-food-eating contest?" said Chris Burbank the next day at school. "How would it work?"

Class hadn't started yet. We were all milling around the room. All except Wendell Rice, that is. He was sitting at his desk, checking his homework for the fiftieth time. There was a scowl of concentration on his face, but I could tell he was listening to us, too.

"Well, it would kind of be like a walkathon," I explained. "We'd make a lot of gross, disgusting foods, and people would sponsor us to eat them. They'd pay a certain amount per plate. Five dollars, say. That way, if someone ate six platefuls, their sponsor would pay—"

"Thirty dollars," Wendell interrupted.

"I *know* that, Wendell," I said. "Anyway, I think we could get a lot of money with a gross-food-eating contest, and it would be more interesting than selling gift wrap. What do you guys think?"

"*I* think it's a *revolting* idea," Wendell said. "Now, my science contest would be much—"

"*I* think it's a great idea," Elayne Munter cut in. "I don't want to eat anything gross myself," she added hastily. "Maybe I could just count plates or something."

"What would we have to eat?" asked another girl.

"Nothing poisonous, of course," I said. "Nothing rotten, and no worms or insects. Maybe some gross combinations. Chicken soup with maple syrup, or—"

"Tortilla chips with salsa and chocolate pudding," said Chris Burbank, his eyes shining. "Raw garlic cloves dipped in whipped cream!"

"Pickle-and-jelly-bean sandwiches!" called another kid.

"Soft-boiled eggs with sugar lumps and anchovies!"

"English muffins!"

We all stared at Noelle Lanni, who had made the last suggestion. "What's wrong with English muffins?" I asked.

Noelle shrugged. "I just don't like them, that's all."

"This is a great idea," said Chris Burbank excitedly. "Now that you're not such a nerd, Sam, you're really starting to be a normal person." (That was a big compliment, coming from Chris.)

I could see that the rest of my class was also getting excited about the idea. I was sure the other fifth-graders would like it, too. All we had to do was get permission.

That turned out to be easy, once we promised the teachers two things: that we would hold the contest out on the playground and that we'd clean up the mess ourselves. "Also, I'm not watching while you eat soft-boiled eggs," said our teacher, Miss Swang. "*I* think soft-boiled eggs are the most disgusting food on the planet, with or without sugar lumps."

"I assume Stanley's going to be involved in this gross-food-eating contest," Marjorie said after school.

"Well, of course he is," I said. "For Stanley, it will be like going to a fancy restaurant. He'll be in heaven."

"And where will *you* be?" Marjorie asked suspiciously. "Standing next to him, eating *your* share of gross foods?"

"Of course not," I said. "Stanley's going to be substituting for me. Isn't that obvious?"

Marjorie didn't answer for a second. "But aren't you kind of cheating?" she finally said. "You get to skip the contest. We get to eat chocolate meat loaf, or whatever. And the whole thing was *your* idea. Does that seem fair?"

I had to admit, I hadn't looked at it that way. All I had been thinking about was how much fun a contest like this would be, and how famous it would make me.

"It's—it's too late to worry about it now," I faltered. "I mean, everyone wants to have the contest. We can't call it off! Besides, think how much money it will raise for the school," I added. "That's more important than having to eat a few foods you don't like, isn't it?"

Marjorie just looked at me. "Okay. I'll help you clean up Stanley so he'll look like you. But I'll only do it if *you* promise to eat some gross stuff, too. You've got to suffer along with the rest of us."

"What do you think of this poster?" Suzannah Flor asked me one afternoon a week later. It was after school, and we were all working on publicity posters in the media center. (All except Wendell, of course.)

Suzannah's poster had a big muddy-looking blob in the middle. Above it were the words EAT TILL YOU PUKE!

"What's that stuff?" I asked. "Soup?"

"No way!" said Suzannah. "It's barf! Neat, huh?"

Barf as advertising. An interesting idea, I thought.

Besides making posters, we also made an announcement about the contest on the P.A. system in the principal's office. It was great. It started out with Chris Burbank making a horrible hacking sound.

"Oh, my," said Elayne politely. "Are you sick?"

"Nope," Chris answered. "Just bringing up a little phlegm for the Gross-Food-Eating Contest."

"Fabulous! What are you serving it with?"

"Oh, I thought I'd put it on cinnamon toast. But there are plenty of other neat combinations at the contest, too. Come on and grab a plate, everyone!"

Now, tell me that doesn't make you want to drop everything and run to the contest.

Collecting sponsors for the contest was a lot harder than doing publicity. My parents were hopeless, of course. No *way* would they ever sponsor me to eat platefuls of cinnamon toast with phlegm. And their accountant friends weren't the kind of people who'd want to help out, either. I tried going door to door—that didn't work too well, either.

Finally I had the idea of going over to the university where my uncle Zachary works. I hate to brag, but that was *perfect*. All the college kids loved the idea. The only problem was that *every single* college student who sponsored me said, "Gee, you should use the food from the dining hall here. It's gross enough!" You get tired of laughing at the same joke five hundred times.

*   *   *

Unfortunately, training Stanley to substitute for me was even harder than collecting sponsors.

The three of us—Stanley, Marjorie, and I—had a little practice session every day after school up in the tree house. First we would practice wearing my school clothes, since of course Stanley would have to be dressed just like me. We had dressed Stanley up once before—at a party my parents gave—but he still hated it. "Pants too *ouch*," he kept complaining, trying to yank them off. Stanley's favorite outfit is an oversize T-shirt that Uncle Zach washes for him once in a while.

"Samuel, I thought I told you always to change out of your school clothes before you go out to play!" my mother complained one night, wrinkling her nose. "These pants look as if they've been rolled in bird droppings!" I didn't tell her that *was* what had happened to them. Stanley had been hoping that I'd forget about his wearing school clothes if he messed them up enough.

In addition to clothes-wearing, we also practiced walking in a straight line without getting distracted. That was a tough one, too. Stanley was always dashing off to hunt for grubs.

Next Marjorie and I worked on getting Stanley to talk like me. Since we couldn't predict what the kids at school might talk about, we tried to prepare Stanley for everything.

"Stanley, pretend someone asks if you have a lot of homework," I said. "What will you say?"

"Yes! Miss Swang am doodoo-head!" Stanley told me brightly.

"Okay, Stanley," Marjorie said the next afternoon. "Someone asks who you want to win the World Series. What's your answer?"

"Uh . . . Uncle Zach?" Stanley asked. We just shook our heads.

"Stanley, one thing you'll be asked for sure is how many sponsors you got for this contest," I said the next afternoon. "Just tell them thirty-five, okay?"

"Okay, Sam," Stanley said confidently. "A hundredy-forty-o'leven."

Finally I told him not to talk at all. "Just walk up to the table and start eating," I said. "*That* shouldn't be too hard."

Stanley nodded. "Eat lots," he said confidently. Then he yanked up his T-shirt and started playing with his belly-button lint. Stanley has so much belly-button lint that you practically can't *see* his belly button under it.

I squeezed my eyes shut quickly. "And speaking of things you shouldn't do in front of other people . . ."

"It's a health menace," mumbled Wendell in a muffled voice. He was pressing a handkerchief over his nose and staring down at the tables covered with contest foods.

The afternoon of the contest was here at last. School had let out a half an hour before and we had just finished setting everything up on the playground. Now we were all waiting behind the food tables while the audience sat down.

Big, festive banners that said THE GROSS-FOOD-EATING CONTEST and SWALLOW IT! were draped around the swing set and were hung from the basketball hoop. All the fifth-graders were wearing sashes with the names of the foods they'd contributed to the feast. (Mine said "Mom's Home Cooking." It was one of Mom's favorite recipes—Sweet 'n' Sour Franks 'n' Beans. She didn't know, of course.) We had brought out all the chairs from the lunchroom and set them in rows in front of the food tables so that everyone would get a good view. (If they *wanted* a good view.)

Pretty much the whole school had stayed to watch the big event, including our principal, Mrs. Carp. It wasn't really her kind of thing, but she'd been sort of a friend of mine ever since I protected her from a flying lobster shell Wendell accidentally threw at her. Our gym teacher was there, too, and of course Miss Swang. She looked pretty unhappy. "But I'm certainly proud of them for being so *inventive*," I heard her telling another teacher.

"Have you thought about rats, Samuel?" Wendell continued. "This food will attract hordes of them, you know. It's terrifically unsanitary."

"Oh, be quiet, Wendell," said Kim Fenton crossly. "We all washed our hands before we cooked anything. Besides, I don't see a single rat, do you?"

It was true. Maybe the food was so gross that it even scared *rats* away. (If there *were* any rats around in the first place.) The food-covered tables looked like those paintings that four-year-olds make, with horrible clashing colors and drips and blobs and smears all over. And whatever the opposite of air-freshener is, it smelled as though someone had sprayed it all over the playground.

"Attention, please! Attention, please!" our announcer, a fifth-grader named Darwell Ringer, shouted through a megaphone. "Will everybody please sit down? Let the little kids have the seats in front. Sixth-graders, please sit in the back." (All the big, tough sixth-grade kids had pushed to the front, of course.) "The contest will not start until the little kids can see." Darwell looked as if he liked bossing the sixth-graders around.

Squealing with excitement, the little kids rushed toward the chairs in front. (Grumbling, the older kids slowly moved toward the back.) "I love that plate there!" I heard one kindergarten girl say, pointing to a red-and-white mess on a green plate. "It looks like Christmas!"

When everyone was sitting down again, and we

fifth-graders had settled into our special VIP section, Darwell picked up the megaphone. "And now, our contest will begin," he boomed. "The first contestant is . . . is . . ."

He looked around nervously. "Who *is* the first contestant?" he asked in a stage whisper. "Did we pick someone?"

"Come on. Who's going to be first?" Wendell asked with a sneer. "I can't wait to see you all make yourselves sick."

No one stepped forward.

No one stepped forward again.

We all looked around.

The sixth-graders began to whoop. "GO! GO! GO! BARF! BARF! BARF!" they chanted, stamping their feet.

"Who's Bart?" I heard another kindergartner ask.

"This is *very* inspiring," Wendell sneered.

Finally Chris Burbank cleared his throat. "Might as well get it over with," he croaked.

He picked up a fork, closed his eyes, and dipped the fork into the nearest plate, which the sign said was canned snails covered with butterscotch frosting and stuffed inside jumbo olives.

"Go, Chris! You can do it, Chris!" everyone in the audience started cheering.

"It's not too gross for you!" Chris's third-grade brother called out encouragingly. "Remember the time you ate that peanut butter and spaghetti sandwich?"

"Hold your breath and you'll be fine!"

"Wash it down with some water!"

Chris's eyes flew open when the snail touched his tongue. A look of horror crossed his face. He chewed once—kind of with the tips of his teeth, if you know what I mean—and then swallowed hard. We could all see a big snaily bulge traveling down his throat.

"Yay, Chris!" Elayne Munter said in a thin, scared voice. She was sitting on a stool next to the food tables so she could take good notes. "Come on, finish the plate! You can do it!"

Well, Chris did manage to finish the plate of snails. Then he ate a plateful of sardine-flavored brownies, a fried egg rolled up around some grapes stuffed with clam dip, and a raw onion smeared with lard. *Then* he gave us sort of a wobbly look and asked, "Does it count if you throw up?"

"I—I don't think so," I said. "I think it has to stay in your stomach for your sponsors to pay you."

"Then I'd better stop now," said Chris, and he lay down right on the blacktop.

Things didn't get much better after that. Good old Marjorie managed a plate of cat food ice cream, and lots of other fifth-graders took a turn after her. But most of them could only manage one bite of anything. Elayne Munter tried to get us to change the rules so that it counted if you just sniffed each plate, but no one else thought that was fair.

The audience was getting restless. "This is stupid, Miss Martin," one first-grade girl complained to her teacher. "They're being babies!"

Wendell heard her and let out a hoot of derision. "Looks as though you've raised about five dollars," he said. "That ought to buy one twig for the school yard." His eyes scanned the crowd sneeringly.

"Don't give up hope," Marjorie said calmly. "Sam hasn't had his turn yet."

Everyone turned to stare at me.

"Well?" Wendell asked. "Aren't you going to try some of these delicious foods, Samuel? This whole thing was your idea, after all."

"Of course I'm going to try them," I said stoutly. I stood up and walked over to the tables.

"Here he is!" Darwell shouted. "The one and only Sam Moore! The famous thinker-up of the contest."

"Big whoop," one of the sixth-graders called from the back.

I stared down at the food for a second. Then, while my stomach lurched around in horror, I picked up a lard-covered onion and popped it into my mouth.

Lard is a lot like Vaseline going down, I realized. I smiled at the audience as best I could.

"This really whets my appetite," I said thickly. "I'll just try a few more bites before I decide which plate to start with."

It was even harder to smile when I tried the tuna-marshmallow whip and the chicken in chocolate syrup, but I was determined to make Wendell believe in me. "These bites don't count," I said at last. "Now that I've practiced, I'm ready for some *real* eating. Just let me go to the bathroom first. I mean, I plan to be at this table for some time!"

"No fair throwing up!" a sixth-grade girl called from the back of the audience.

"Of course not!" I protested. "Don't you trust me?" I raced into the school.

Stanley and I had made our final plans before school that morning. Just as we had planned, he was waiting for me in the boys' bathroom on the first floor. (Luckily everyone else was out on the playground.) He was drinking out of the toilet. "Sam! Me hun'ry!" he wailed when he saw me. A big trickle of drool gushed out of his mouth. "Want foo!"

I laughed. "You're about to get all the food you want," I told him. Quickly I grabbed a paper towel and gave his face a final dust-off. Then I took him by the shoulders and stared into his crusty eyes.

"Now, Stanley. What are you going to remember?"

"No talk," Stanley said. "On'y eat lots foo."

"And what do you do when you're done?"

"I right back here. No stop see garbage cans!"

"That's right," I told him. "Good luck. I know you'll do a fantastic job!"

Stanley started to lick my forehead goodbye, but I shoved him out the door. Then I peeked out the window to watch his progress.

Stanley loped across the playground eagerly. When he spotted the tables, he gave a whoop of delight. Spreading his arms like an eagle, he went crashing through the audience as he charged toward the food.

Kids scrambled frantically to get out of his path. I don't think Stanley even saw them. He was staring too hard at the food.

When he reached the first table, he squatted down in front of a plate of hot dog cupcakes and opened his mouth wide. Then he started sucking them in like a vacuum cleaner.

The cupcakes were gone in twenty seconds.

Everyone cheered when the plate was empty. "Amazing, Moore!" I heard Chris Burbank yell. Alone in the bathroom I smiled proudly.

Stanley moved on to the next plate, which was heaped with raw mushrooms stuffed with gumdrops. In a few more seconds that plate, too, was empty. Stanley only paused to lick it clean before he moved on to the next dish.

Everyone was staring at him with their hands

over their mouths. Elayne Munter was doubled up with disgust. And Wendell Rice looked ready to pop, he was so mad.

In fewer than five minutes all four tables were empty of everything except licked-clean plates. For good measure Stanley had even inhaled all the bits of food that had fallen onto the ground. That meant cleanup would be really easy—which was a relief to me, since I knew I wouldn't be able to help. (I felt guilty about that. But I didn't want to push my luck with all this switching back and forth. As soon as Stanley was cleaned up, I wanted him *out* of there.)

I squinted through the window to see Elayne Munter frantically adding up numbers on her notepad. After a few more seconds she shouted, "Ladies and—I mean, listen, guys! Sam Moore just ate forty-five platefuls of gross food! So let's give Sam a big, big—"

Burp. A big, big burp. It came from Stanley.

And it practically blew everyone across the playground.

CHAPTER THREE

Burger Trouble

You know, it's funny. All the gross-food eating hadn't made anyone sick. I mean, no one actually barfed, even though a few kids were on the *edge* of barfing.

That wave of hot, horrible, burp-air pushed Wendell right over the edge, though.

Wendell had never sat down with the rest of the kids. He had hovered at the edge of the contest, disgusted but unable to tear himself away.

Now, as the burp-air hit him, Wendell's face turned greenish gray. A thin trickle of liquid started leaking out both sides of his mouth.

"Watch out!" called Chris Burbank. "Rice is gonna blow chunks! Move out of range!"

"Gettin' ready to drive the porcelain bus," Teri Hermann added with a giggle.

"You mean yawn in color," Nan Leiland corrected her.

"Spew," someone else contributed.

"Share his lunch."

"Call it what you want, as long as he doesn't do it on *me*."

"Get it under control, dude!" Chris Burbank called.

But Wendell was too far gone for that. He bent over and retched. I felt a little sorry for him. It's so embarrassing throwing up in front of your whole school.

"Hurl into the *creek*, Rice!" Todd Garfinkle shouted. "Not *here* in *front* of us!" Impatiently he added, "Trust Rice to wimp out on us. He should have joined the contest. That would have toughened him up."

Wendell lurched across the playground toward the creek. Halfway there he started throwing up again. But there was still lots of barf left inside him once he got to the creek.

"Oh, well," Elayne Munter said. "It's supposed to rain tonight."

In all the excitement it was easy for Stanley to slip away and bounce up through the open bathroom window without being noticed. After all, the person most likely to have noticed him was busy feeding the fish.

Stanley was glowing with pride. "Me eat lots foo!" he crowed. "D'lishus! Egg! Snail! Mess!"

"It sounds great," I lied. "I'm really proud of you. Now let's clean you off and get out of here."

I jammed the door with the handle of a mop that had been standing in one corner of the bathroom. Then I stood Stanley in a sink and scraped him down with wet paper towels. By the time he was clean, the sink was completely filled with globby washed-off food. It took so long to get *that* clean that I wished I had cleaned Stanley off in one of the toilets. He would've had a great time.

When I finished "washing" Stanley, I dressed him in a fresh set of clothes I'd stashed in the bathroom earlier. (I hadn't bothered to make this outfit identical to mine.) Then I tried to clean his hair a little.

"Me hun'ry," Stanley said as I picked bits of anchovy off his head. "Egg? Snails?"

"Stanley, you *can't* be hungry again!" I said. "I'm the one who's hungry this time!" Starving, actually. It was almost five o'clock, and with all the preparations for the contest, I hadn't even had time to eat lunch.

Stanley gave a big, wet, snoggly sniff. Slimy green tears leaked out of his eyes and dribbled onto his shirt like drops of green glue.

"Okay, okay. We'll stop at a fast-food place on the way home," I said. "I'll get us a couple of cheeseburgers. But you'll have to wait out back where nobody can see you."

"I wait, Sam," my twin said cheerfully. He rubbed his green-smeared face on his sleeve—so much for clean clothes!—and followed me out the door.

A couple of blocks later we reached the Burger

Barn. I led Stanley around to the back. "Stay here until I come out for you," I warned him. "I'll be back as soon as I can. And don't play in the Dumpster while I'm gone."

The Burger Barn makes really great stuff. I ordered two cheeseburgers for myself, and two cheeseburgers with double everything for Stanley. *His* cheeseburgers looked like worm guts, but mine looked great. I couldn't resist taking a huge bite as I fumbled in my pocket for my money.

"Hungry so soon?" came a familiar voice from behind me.

I froze. I even stopped chewing.

Wendell Rice had followed me into the restaurant.

I should tell you here that Wendell—who had considered me his best friend until a food fight in the lunchroom—was very suspicious of me and Stanley. He had caught a glimpse of Stanley during the food fight, when Stanley had thrown some rotten eggs into his face. Marjorie and I had managed to whisk Stanley out of the way, but I knew that *Wendell* knew something strange was going on. Even if he didn't know exactly what it was.

"Mmmmmffff," I said quickly now. I swallowed the lump of cheeseburger in my mouth and dropped the rest of the burger into my take-out bag. "Oh, hi, Wendell," I said, trying to sound casual. "Are you feeling better?"

"Somewhat. No thanks to you," Wendell said coldly.

"Sorry," I said. "You shouldn't eat here, then."

"I *never* eat here," Wendell replied, curling his lip. "Fast food is high in fat and sodium. I saw you through the window and decided to come in to say hello."

"Oh. Well, hello. And—uh—g'bye!"

I plopped the money on the counter and started toward the door—but Wendell stepped in front of me.

"*Why* are you so hungry, Samuel?" he asked suspiciously. "Back at the contest you ate enough to kill a horse."

"I guess I worked up an appetite with all that chewing," I said quickly. "And, uh, I needed to eat some normal food after all that *gross* stuff. You know, the way you can always eat dessert no matter how much other stuff you eat." I was on a roll now, I thought. "And," I went on, "cheeseburgers were the normalest thing I could—"

"Sam? *Sam?* SAM! *SAM!* SAAAAAAAAA-AAAM!"

I froze again. It was *another* familiar voice. And I bet you can guess whose voice it was. Everyone in the place turned around to watch Stanley bursting through the door.

"I *knew* it," said Wendell under his breath. "I knew there was more than one of you at that food fight."

Stanley didn't see Wendell at first. "Sam!

Burgers!" he bellowed as he charged toward me. "Burgers! BUR—"

Then he caught sight of Wendell.

"—gers," he finished in a quieter bellow.

I took a deep breath. "Wendell," I said, "I'd like you to meet my . . . cousin. My cousin Stanley."

"Pleased of meet at you," said Stanley. He dug his thumb into his nose, then stuck that same hand out to Wendell. But Wendell didn't shake it. Eyes narrowed, he was staring at Stanley.

"He looks like more than a cousin," he said.

"We're identical cousins," I said quickly. "Our fathers were identical twins."

Stanley was standing there picking his teeth with his fingernail. He dug out one especially tender morsel from behind a molar and popped it into his mouth.

"There's no such thing as identical cousins." Wendell was still squinting at Stanley as if he were something on the bottom of his shoe. "Where does he live?"

"In tree," Stanley blurted out.

"Tree, Montana," I improvised. "It's a very small—"

All at once Stanley interrupted. "Burger!" he shouted eagerly. I had set the bag on a table behind me, and I guess Stanley had just noticed it.

He tore the bag open, grabbed one of his cheeseburgers, and crammed the whole thing into his mouth. One huge gulp, and it was gone.

(Except for a river of ketchup, mustard, and pickle relish that blurpled out onto his chin.) He did the same thing with his second cheeseburger. He was reaching for one of *my* burgers when Wendell spoke again.

"That's the same revolting way you crammed in that food at the contest, Samuel," he said. "Or *was* that you?"

Uh-oh. "Of course that was me!" I did my best to give a hearty laugh. "I wouldn't let my favorite cousin eat gross stuff like that, would I?"

"It not gross! It pretty!" Stanley objected.

"Stanley's such a goofball." I laughed my fake laugh again. "Well, we'd better get home. Stanley's catching a plane back to Tree in a few minutes. G'bye!"

I grabbed Stanley's hand and yanked him out the door, leaving my cheeseburgers on the table.

Stanley seemed to realize that he had gotten me into trouble. He let me take him back to his tree house without fussing. He didn't even mention the forgotten cheeseburgers. When I said goodbye, he was quietly playing on the floor with his turtle.

My parents weren't home from work yet, so I had plenty of time to walk around the house worrying. How much did Wendell know? Was there any way he could mess things up for Stanley? What if he told people that it was Stanley, not me, who had eaten that food? Would anyone believe him?

When my parents pulled into the driveway, it was actually a relief. And usually the sight of my parents is anything *but* a relief.

Mom and Dad are pretty weird. I know that most kids think their parents are weird, but my mom and dad really are. My mother worries nine hundred percent more than the average mother, and she cooks things that no fifth-grader would want to swallow—even in a gross-food contest. She also has this very obnoxious, boring Persian cat named Creamy that she treats like she's my little sister.

My dad talks like a stern father out of an old book, and both my parents call me by my full name—Samuel.

And both of them were too excited when they got home to notice how worried I was.

"Samuel! Samuel!" my mother trilled as she raced through the front door. She bent to give Creamy a pat, then turned to me. "Look at this!"

In her hand was a copy of the *Elmwood Eagle*, our evening newspaper.

My heart jumped into my throat. For a second I was afraid that the headline would say something like FIFTH-GRADER'S WEIRD TWIN INFLICTS PLAYGROUND INJURIES WITH MASSIVE BELCH.

What I saw instead was a photograph of my uncle Zachary.

"That's not about me!" I gasped like a total moron.

"Of course it isn't, dear," said my mother. "It's about Uncle Zachary. *My* little brother! Samuel, Zachary has won the Pinkerton Prize! Oh, I'm over the moon!"

Now that my heart wasn't hammering so hard, I could read what the headline actually said:

ELMWOOD CHEMISTRY PROFESSOR HONORED WITH INTERNATIONAL AWARD.

Under the headline was a long article about how Dr. Zachary Oshrain, Ph.D., had won the Pinkerton Prize for his remarkable cloning experiments.

"Oshrain's success at cloning plants may lead to future experiments with animal life," the article ended. "Many of his techniques were perfected in his basement laboratory at the home of his sister, Mrs. Milton Moore.

"Asked if he might ever consider cloning humans, the world-famous scientist gave a strange laugh. 'That kind of experiment can go way too far,' he said."

Right, I thought. *It sure can. And you and I both know how much too far it can go, Uncle Zach.*

Don't get me wrong. I was really happy that my uncle had won the prize. I was also very fond of Stanley. But right at that moment I wished that Uncle Zach had become a world-famous poet or fire fighter or something.

Anything except a scientist who went around creating identical twins that got nephews into trouble.

"Your attention, please!" It was Mrs. Carp, our principal, speaking over the P.A. system the next morning. "We've just finished our final tally, and I'm proud to announce that the fifth grade has won the fund-raising contest with their Gross-Food-Eating Contest. The third-graders came in second with their masking-tape sale. Congratulations to all for a fine effort!"

Everyone in my class burst into cheers.

"Fifth grade *rules*!" Elayne Munter squealed.

"I'm so proud of you, people," said Miss Swang. "You all did a fabulous job."

"Sam should get most of the credit," Chris Burbank said. "It was all his idea. He ate the most food, too."

I glanced over at Wendell. I was sure he was going to spill the beans. I didn't think anyone would believe him, but I wanted to be ready.

To my surprise, though, Wendell didn't say a word. He just slitted his eyes and stared meanly at me. Then he turned back toward Miss Swang.

"Samuel has some exciting news from home, too," he told her. "I read about it in the newspaper." He leered at me. "Wouldn't you like to tell the class about your uncle?"

What was Wendell up to now? I wondered.

"What's your news, Sam?" asked Miss Swang kindly.

I looked Wendell in the eye—hard. "My uncle won a big prize yesterday," I said. "For some experiments he's done."

"Some *cloning* experiments," Wendell said in a meaningful voice. "I knew Dr. Oshrain was a scientist, but Samuel never mentioned that he did work with cloning."

"How interesting! Could you explain to the class what cloning is, Sam?" asked Miss Swang.

I knew what it was—all too well!—but I didn't exactly know how to explain it. "It's sort of like when you make exact copies of things," I said, trying to sound casual. "Like Uncle Zachary will take one plant and clone it—make a new plant that's exactly the same."

"Has he ever cloned a person?" asked Wendell slyly.

If I'd been wondering before what Wendell was up to, I was sure now. He didn't know for certain that Stanley was a clone, but he was suspicious—and he wanted me to see that he was on my trail.

"Scientists can't clone people," I said firmly. "At least, not yet. You should know *that*, Wendell. Don't you read science magazines?"

"Maybe someday they will," said Miss Swang.

"Won't that be exciting?"

I thought it was exciting enough already. Too exciting, actually.

But wait. Let me end one part of the suspense right here. Wendell never did spill the beans about my "cousin" from "Tree." For a week after the contest we all collected the money from our sponsors and put it with the money the other grades had raised. Then we had a big meeting about how to spend it. The teachers wouldn't approve a wave machine, but they did let us order a video camera that anyone could check out of the media center.

"So I guess it all came out okay," said Marjorie after school on the day the video camera arrived.

I guess that depends on what you mean by "okay."

A few days later, when I got home from school, I heard Uncle Zachary talking to someone in his lab. Was it Stanley? I wondered as I pushed the lab door open and walked in.

I stopped in my tracks. No, the person Uncle Zach was talking to wasn't Stanley.

"Hey, dude!" said Uncle Zach happily. "I'd like you to meet my new research assistant. He's a friend of yours, isn't he?"

"Well, we *know* each other," I said flatly.

It was Wendell Rice.

CHAPTER FOUR

Wendell Makes Himself at Home

"I'm sure you know that Wendell is very interested in science, Sam," said Uncle Zachary.

"Especially cloning," said Wendell with a smile.

"That's right!" said my uncle brightly. "He's volunteered to help me with some of my cloning experiments. Sam, Wendell likes lab stuff, just like you. Won't it be nice to have a friend around in the afternoons?"

Nice? I gave Wendell a hate-filled stare. He was wearing a new white lab coat I wished I could rub dirt on.

"How did you beat me home from school?" I asked.

"I had my mother drive me." Wendell smirked. "She's going to pick me up and bring me here every day from now on. Perhaps you'd like to have a ride, too?"

"No, thanks," I muttered. "I like the bus."

Uncle Zachary is such a nice guy that I don't think he noticed the tension in the room. "Hey,

Sam, how about helping me show Wendell around the lab?" he asked.

"Thank you, Dr. Oshrain," said Wendell politely.

I even wanted to punch him for saying *that*.

Uncle Zachary's lab isn't one of those white, sterile, gleaming places you see on TV. He never cleans anything up. When he finishes an experiment, he just shoves it to one side until it's so moldy he can't stand it anymore. (Anyone who didn't know Uncle Zachary might think he *tries* to grow mold.)

I could tell that Wendell was a little shocked at how messy everything was. He kept sniffing as though he smelled something bad. He also kept running his finger along tabletops and stuff to check for dust. He *also* kept trying to read the stuff on Uncle Zach's desk. He even asked Uncle Zach what was inside his desk drawers.

"Just paperwork," Uncle Zach told him. "Nothing you'd be interested in."

"May I read it sometime? I'd *love* to see what a great scientist thinks and writes," said Wendell in an oozy voice.

Uncle Zach laughed a little. "Honest, there's nothing good to read in there."

Wendell didn't say anything more, but I noticed that his gaze kept sneaking over to my uncle's desk. He kept looking at the closets, too. Was he wondering whether Stanley was inside?

"This is a lot more fun than paperwork," Uncle Zach went on. He pushed aside an old mildewed blanket and uncovered a remote-control model car.

"You don't *play* in your lab, I hope," Wendell said.

Uncle Zach just grinned. "Not exactly," he said. "I'm experimenting with fuels. I've given that car an engine with perpetual fuel-regeneration capability. It regenerates all the fuel it needs, over and over."

"But what *for*?" Wendell whined. "It's just a toy!"

Wendell never understands the *practical* side of things. He may be a genius, but he's not smart about the real world.

"It's more than a toy," I corrected him. "If you could put a self-fueling engine into a regular car, you could save fuel and cut down on pollution. Right, Uncle Zach?"

Wendell glared at me. I could tell he was mad that I had figured something out before he did.

"Exactly, Sam," said Uncle Zach. "One of these days we'll see if it works with full-size engines. Here's one of my cloning experiments," he went on, pointing to a row of glass slides on a counter. "Part of it, anyway. Those are tissue samples from some cacti I cloned."

"Fascinating," Wendell said eagerly. "And now, what experiment would you like me to start with? Cloning?"

"Whoa, dude!" said Uncle Zachary with a chuckle. "How about something a little simpler? Like cleaning up some of these papers?" He pointed to a huge, messy pile of crumpled-up newspapers in one corner. "And then maybe you could scrub out the spider tank for me. Make sure you get all the droppings out of the corners. And after that—well, we'll see. Maybe I'll let you take notes for me while *I* do some experiments. Kind of ease you into things."

Wendell's shoulders drooped disappointedly, but he didn't say anything. I guess he didn't want to make a fuss on his first day at work.

Well, if he was going to be cleaning up for a while, it was probably safe for me to do my homework. But first I needed to talk to my uncle.

"Uncle Zach, could you come up to my room for a second?" I asked. "I need some help with my math."

"*I'd* be glad to help, Samuel," Wendell offered. "Mathematics is one of my best subjects, you know."

"No, thanks" was what I said. *I can't believe what a weasel you are* was what I thought.

"That was nice of Wendell to offer to help you," said Uncle Zachary cheerfully when we were up in my room. "I think it's going to be fun having him around, don't you?"

I just stared at him. "Are you kidding, Uncle Zach? Don't you see what a loser he is? He's like my least favorite kid at school! I mean, I used to feel sorry for him, but he's got a totally awful personality!"

As I said before, Uncle Zachary is so nice that he never sees anything wrong with other people. I suppose that's a good way to be—but not when you don't see anything wrong with *Wendell*.

"Didn't you hear how Wendell wrecked Mom and Dad's whole party?" I asked. "They hate him now."

"Now, Sam, I'm sure he's sorry about that," said Uncle Zach.

"But—but, Uncle Zach, Wendell knows about *Stanley*!" I sputtered. Quickly I explained what had happened after the gross-food-eating contest. "I'm sure he's trying to sniff Stanley out," I finished. "He's up to something. I just know it!"

Uncle Zachary chuckled. "Well, he shouldn't have much trouble sniffing Stanley out."

"But he'll tell *everyone* about Stanley if he finds him!" I protested. "I know he will! He'll—he'll say something like, 'The world of science must know of this discovery!' And then Stanley will have to go live in some government lab somewhere, or at Sea World or something!"

Uncle Zach still didn't look worried. "So I'll make sure to keep Wendell away from the tree house," he said. "I really don't think we have a problem here, Sam. All Wendell is doing is helping me take notes on my experiments. And cleaning up the lab a little. Have a little faith. He's kind of nerdy, but I'm sure he's a good kid at heart."

I could see it was no use trying to change my uncle's mind. So I called Marjorie and told her everything. "I'm positive Wendell's looking for Stanley," I said. "I'm sure that's the real reason he asked Uncle Zach for a job."

"Do you think Stanley will stay in his tree house?" Marjorie asked. "He likes to visit the lab sometimes, doesn't he?" She sounded worried.

"Yes. We're going to have to keep him away." I sighed. "I don't know *how*, though. He'll get bored in his tree house all alone. We should start teaching him to read."

"Good idea. I'll try to think up some arts and crafts and stuff for him, too," Marjorie offered. "Some of the things we used to do in Brownies might work. Weaving pot holders, for instance . . ."

Her voice trailed off. I could tell she was imagining the kind of pot holders someone like Stanley would make.

"Mrs. Moore, these rutabagas are absolutely delicious. Might I trouble you for a second helping?" asked Wendell a couple of hours later.

"Hmmmmph," my mother muttered under her breath as she passed him another spoonful.

Suppertime with Wendell. What fun. About as much fun as washing Uncle Zach's moldy petri dishes.

My parents used to think Wendell was the

ideal child. In lots of ways, it would have worked out better if *he* had been their son instead of me. He's such a world-class nerd that they all would have been happy.

But then Wendell barged in on a party Mom and Dad were giving for a group of accountants and started shouting that one of my mom's weird foods was toxic waste. They weren't too crazy about him after that.

So when Uncle Zachary invited Wendell to stay for supper at my house, the only person who was happy was Wendell. I think Mom let him stay only because she was so proud of Uncle Zachary for winning the award. At that point she would have done anything for her little brother.

Wendell was doing his best to butter up my parents, I noticed. First there was all that talk about the food. Even *Wendell* can't really love rutabagas. Or chicken burgers with carrot ketchup. Or pickled-ginger pudding.

He gobbled it all down, though. "That was utterly delicious, Mrs. Moore," he said when he was done. "And how's your brother, Mr. Moore?" he asked.

"My brother?" Dad said with a puzzled look. "Fine, thanks." And he went on talking to my mother about one of their clients.

Wendell looked disappointed. Dad really does have a brother. He doesn't have an identical twin brother, the way I told Wendell, but Wendell

didn't know that. The secret of my "cousin" was at least a teeny bit safer now.

"I guess I'd better take you home, dude," said Uncle Zachary when the meal was over. "I've got to get back to my apartment. Thanks for dinner!" he said to my mother.

"You're welcome. Come again soon," said my mother fondly. "And, Zach—we're so, so proud of you for winning that award. My brother—a *genius*!"

She didn't even look at Wendell.

So Wendell made one last try to get her attention. On his way out he noticed Creamy dozing in the living room. (She's always either sleeping, eating, or sneezing.)

"Oh, I *always* look forward to seeing that beautiful cat," said Wendell. He bent down to pat her.

With a high-pitched yowl, Creamy leaped up and scratched Wendell on the nose.

Good, I thought. *Creamy doesn't like you, either.*

If *everyone* who lived in my house wanted Wendell out of the way, what could he do but go?

CHAPTER FIVE

Glop and More Glop

"Now, Stanley, this is called play dough," explained Marjorie patiently. She set a big bowl full of homemade play dough on the floor of Stanley's tree house. "You can use it to make all kinds of things."

"P'aydough," Stanley repeated. "It pretty!" He scooped up a handful of play dough and smeared it over his head. Another handful he packed into his nose. Then he looked hopefully over at Marjorie. "Like that, Mawyahnee?" he asked, blowing a plug of play dough from each nostril.

Marjorie sighed and glanced over at me. "Am I crazy to be doing this?" she asked.

"I don't know," I answered. "Maybe you'll discover the secret artist hidden in Stanley's soul."

Or maybe not. The next time I looked at Stanley, he was grabbing handfuls of play dough and squeezing them through his fingers. He laughed every time a blob plopped onto the floor.

Marjorie and I had already started teaching Stanley his letters. He especially loved the alphabet book I'd made for him. "A is for Awful," it began. "B is for Bore. C is for Caterpillar squished on the floor. . . ." I'm sure you get the idea. I'd found Stanley poring over his alphabet a lot already. "*P* am for Puke," he'd murmur. "*R* am for Roach. . . ." He was such a quick learner that I knew he'd be reading real books soon.

Sometimes, when I'd check on my twin, I'd find him sleeping. Stanley could fall sound asleep wherever he happened to be sitting—or standing. Once I found him leaning up against the wall taking a nap. I finally figured out that all of Stanley's "extra" talents—bouncing, slithering under doors, and so on—used so much energy that he needed more sleep than an ordinary person.

Today was our first day of tree house arts and crafts. Just as she had promised, Marjorie had brought over some crafts that might make Stanley more interested in staying in his tree house. Besides play dough, finger paints and rubber stamps were scheduled for the afternoon's activities.

Unfortunately, Marjorie had forgotten to bring any smocks. Not that Stanley would have used one. As you've probably figured out by now, he *likes* getting messy. Marjorie and I could have protected ourselves from flying glop if *we* had had smocks, though.

Suddenly a loud, wet sound broke into my thoughts. Stanley had just stuck his head into the bowl of play dough and started licking it.

"Marjorie, you have to keep an eye on him when you're doing a project like this," I said crossly. I grabbed Stanley by the shoulders and pulled him out of the bowl.

"Yeah, like *you* weren't sitting right beside him!" Marjorie snapped.

"No fight! No fight!" Stanley begged us. He grabbed both our heads in his gloppy hands and smushed our noses together. "Friends," he said firmly.

I didn't want to laugh, but I couldn't help it. "Okay, Stanley, you win," I said. I pulled my head out of his grip. "Friends—I'm sorry," I told Marjorie. (Stanley went back to the play dough. First he slapped handfuls of it into his armpits. Then he carefully stuck some more between his toes.) "I'm in a terrible mood. I've got Wendell on the brain. I know he's not supposed to come over today, but I keep worrying that he'll show up anyway."

"But why should he?" said Marjorie. "It's Saturday morning. Wendell only comes over on school days, doesn't he?"

"He's only *supposed* to come over on school days," I said. "But he keeps trying to stay longer each day, and he pokes around Uncle Zach's lab whenever he gets the chance. He keeps wanting to go out into the yard and snoop around, too. He's looking for Stanley. If he keeps on trying so hard, he'll find him for sure."

"Me like he," observed Stanley. He had found the rubber stamps now and was trying to stamp pictures of farm animals on his tongue. "He burger friend." I guess he remembered Wendell from Burger Barn.

"No, Stanley! He's *not* a burger friend! He's not *any* kind of friend!" I said quickly. "If you ever see him around here, you get away. Okay? And don't leave your tree house unless Marjorie or Uncle Zach or I am with you."

Stanley's face fell. "But, Sam! Friend! Want friend!"

"I'm your friend," I told him. "And so's Marjorie. And so's Uncle Zach. All three of us are—"

"Gone!" Stanley interrupted angrily. A slimy green tear dribbled down his dirty face. His frog-like tongue darted out and licked it up. "You am gone lots times! Every day!"

"You have your turtle," I said weakly.

Stanley gave the turtle a doleful look. It was standing quietly in one corner of the tree house. "He not *enough* friend," Stanley told me.

I had to admit I could see what he meant.

"Well, Stanley, Marjorie and I are going to bring you lots and lots of things to do up here." I tried to sound as cheerful as I could. "You'll see. You'll have so much fun learning to read and decorating your tree house with your projects and—uh—taking naps that you won't have time to be lonely."

I hope, I added to myself. Because I wasn't at all sure. Even the messiest bowl of play dough can't take the place of a friend.

That weekend I found a bunch of old first-grade readers up in the attic. I don't know why my mother had saved them. Maybe she thought they were precious heirlooms. Anyway, after school on Monday, Marjorie and I decided to show them to Stanley.

"See, Stanley?" I held up a battered copy of *Animals Are Our Friends* and turned to the first page. "Can you read what the boy is doing?"

Stanley flicked a glance over at the bright, cheerful illustration. It showed a blond boy in neatly ironed clothes pointing at a robin. "Oh, see," the boy was saying. "See the pretty bird. Can the bird come down?"

"Him stupid," Stanley observed, pointing at the boy's smiling face. "Too clean. Bird hate."

"Forget the picture for a second," said Marjorie. "Can you read the *words*?"

Stanley picked up the book. " 'Oh, stink,' " he said. " 'Stink the poopy bird. Can the stinky bird come doodoo?' "

Maybe Stanley was reading the wrong words on purpose. Maybe he thought those were the *right* words. Or maybe he was just making a lucky guess. In any case, Marjorie and I decided to forget about the first-grade readers for now.

They obviously weren't the kind of thing Stanley liked.

"Wendell! What are you doing in my room?" I asked a few days later.

Wendell whipped around to face me. He had been poking through my bedroom closet.

"Oh, hello, Samuel," he said. "I didn't realize you were home from school yet."

I snorted. "No, I can see that. Why are you snooping around my bedroom?"

"Your uncle is missing a few instruments from the lab," Wendell told me coolly. "I thought you might have borrowed them."

"I don't borrow things from the lab," I snapped.

Wendell shrugged. "*I* didn't know that. I just figured that every time you come down and mess up the lab, maybe you help yourself to your uncle's supplies, too."

"What do you mean, mess up the lab?" I asked.

"You know what I mean. I mean that every day when I get here, you've already been to the lab and deliberately tried to make it dirty and disorganized. You know it means I'll have to waste my precious time cleaning up before I can start my real tasks. But it won't work, Samuel. I'll get that lab set up just the way I like it. You'll see."

I pressed my lips tightly together. Of course, Stanley was the one messing up the lab, when he visited Uncle Zach during the day. There was no point in letting Wendell get me mad.

Still, Wendell didn't have to tell me that since he had started working for Uncle Zach, the lab was a changed place. I had heard enough already.

"I don't know how I ever got along without Wendell," Uncle Zachary raved one night when he was having supper at our house. "You can't believe how clean he keeps my lab! All the mold is gone! You can see the floor! He found a missing experiment under the sofa that had been there for three years! Really, he's like a second pair of hands."

"And he's such a smart kid, too," Uncle Zach added. "I never have to explain anything to him twice. I think he understands some of my work better than I do."

"Well, that's nice to hear," said my mother as she heaped my plate with something that looked a lot like Marjorie's play dough. "Maybe I was wrong to be so upset with Wendell. He's certainly been very attentive to Creamy. And I notice that he wears nice, sensible clothing—just like you, Samuel." I was glad Mom didn't know that I changed my clothes after she and Dad left for work.

Every day Wendell made a point of bringing Creamy some kind of treat. To my disgust, he was starting to win her over. She actually purred when she saw him. (She sneezed whenever she saw me.) Sometimes she even padded down the basement stairs to visit him in the lab.

I had been hoping that we would make Wendell so uncomfortable that he'd decide to quit. Instead, I was starting to feel as though, once again, *he* was the one who really belonged in this family. I was just misplaced.

All this flashed through my mind when I found Wendell in my room. It made me furious—especially because I knew what a sleaze he really was. "You know I wouldn't keep lab instruments in my closet," I snapped. "What are you really snooping around for?"

"Well, what do you think, Samuel?"

I stopped short. This wasn't a direction I wanted to go in. *I* sure wasn't going to mention Stanley.

"Anything *you'd* be looking for isn't the kind of thing I'd ever have in my room," I finally said. "Do you think I like the same junk you do?"

"All I think about you," Wendell said loftily, "is that your closet stinks of old sneakers."

I wanted to mash him into the floor like an earwig. "*Out*, Wendell," I growled. "Don't let me catch you up here again."

"And don't let *me* catch you in my garden," Wendell retorted.

"Your garden? What are you talking about?"

"Your uncle asked your parents to let me set up a garden in the backyard," Wendell said

Ann Hodgman

CHAPTER SIX

Cloning Creamy

"It wasn't me, Wendell," I said. Wendell had just arrived and found his garden wrecked. He was standing next to the ruined plants, screaming at me.

"I've been with you all day at school, remember?" I went on. "I haven't been near your stupid garden."

Wendell frowned at me. "If you didn't do it, who did?"

Of course I wasn't going to tell him *that*.

"How should I know?" I said. "It could have been anyone. Some kid from the neighborhood, maybe. Or maybe someone thought it was a bunch of weeds."

"Don't get smart with me, Samuel!" Wendell yelled. "This was a valuable experiment. These were very rare plants. Scientific progress has been destroyed here—"

Suddenly he stopped and stared at the ground. "Look, a clue!" He bent over to look more closely.

"Uh, what kind of clue?" I asked.

"A footprint," said Wendell. "A *bare* footprint." He sniffed. "A smelly footprint," he said, confused.

He pointed. I looked.

There in the dirt, very faint, was the outline of a shoeless foot. And, yes, it did smell pretty gross.

"Hi, guys," came Uncle Zachary's voice from behind us. "How are—Hey! What happened to the plants?"

"You can see for yourself, Dr. Oshrain," said Wendell, putting on a tragic voice. He even had the nerve to wipe a fake tear from his eye.

I didn't say anything. I was staring at the footprint.

It was Stanley's, of course. I knew that right away. And with the evidence in front of me, I could think of only one way to protect my twin.

I took a deep breath. "Gee, Wendell," I said, trying to sound guilty. "I guess you caught me red-handed. Red-footed, I should say."

Wendell and Uncle Zach both stared at me. "Caught *you*?" Wendell began. "But you just said—"

"I know I did," I cut in. "But I didn't expect you to find a clue." I smiled sheepishly at him. "I mean, that *is* my footprint. It's my exact size."

I yanked off my sneaker and pressed my foot down next to the footprint. "See?" I asked. "A perfect match."

As Wendell checked out my feet, Uncle Zachary gave me a sudden look of understanding. He winked at me, then cleared his throat as if he meant business.

"I'm terribly disappointed in you, Sam," he rumbled.

I almost laughed. He sounded so much like someone doing an *imitation* of a stern uncle.

"You know Wendell worked hard on this garden," Uncle Zach went on. "Now you've ruined it."

Wendell tried to break in. "But, Dr. Oshrain, I don't think Samuel's the one who *did* ruin—"

"Of course he did. Who else could it be?"

Wendell didn't answer. I mean, how could he?

"Go up to your room and stay there, Sam," my uncle ordered. "You're lucky I'm not going to tell your mother about this."

He turned to Wendell. "I guess we'll have to keep our work in the lab from now on," he said. "I can see Sam can't be trusted to play out here. Now let's go downstairs."

I smiled as I went up to my room. Uncle Zach might think Wendell was the greatest thing since self-sterilizing test tubes, but he wasn't going to give Stanley away.

"You'd better try to keep Stanley in his tree house," he told me later that evening. "I can't keep an eye on Wendell every second he's around. There are a lot of experiments to work on."

I sighed. "You're right, Uncle Zach. But Stanley's getting bored with his tree house. Luckily he sleeps a lot lately, but I know he wants a friend."

"Maybe this would be the time for Stanley to meet Wendell, then," Uncle Zachary suggested.

"No way!"

"Sam, I really think you can trust Wendell," said my uncle. "He's got a scientific mind. He'd understand. He'd keep the secret, I'm sure. And then Stanley would have another friend besides you and me and Marjorie."

"Uncle Zach, *no*! That wouldn't work!"

"Why not?"

"Because—because—"

I stopped. I had already tried to get Uncle Zach not to like Wendell. It hadn't worked then. It was even less likely to work now that Uncle Zach thought Wendell was so great.

"I just want to train Stanley a little more before he meets other people," I told my uncle. "Give me more time, okay? Stanley's not ready for strangers yet."

Uncle Zachary clapped me on the shoulder. "Whatever makes you happy, Sam," he said. "I'll keep out of this. But I do think Wendell would be a good person to tell."

Well, I don't, I said to myself. And that night, when my parents were asleep, I snuck out to Stanley's tree house. He had left the rope ladder down, and I climbed up.

It didn't surprise me that Stanley was snoring.

If there's a gross sound anywhere in this world, Stanley will make it. I *was* surprised that his snores hadn't knocked the tree house down. They were so loud the whole tree was shaking. When I flicked my flashlight onto his face, I saw that huge spit-bubbles were puffing out of his mouth with each snore.

Also, a bunch of ants were swarming over a sticky spot on his face.

"Stanley! Stanley!" I whispered. I stepped forward and shook his shoulder gently.

Stanley groaned, then burped, and drooled some green stuff onto his pillow. That was how I knew he was awake.

"It's me—Sam," I whispered.

Startled, Stanley sat up in bed, bounced down to the floor, and bounced back onto his bed again. The ants scurried down his neck. "Sam! You come sleep tree house?" Stanley asked.

"No, no. I just wanted to say something. Stanley, that wasn't a good thing you did with Wendell's garden."

Stanley stuck out his lower lip. "Garden yucky," he repeated. "Bad. Mean. Poo—"

"I know you didn't like it," I cut in. "Me, either. But, Stanley, you've got to keep away from the house. You don't want Wendell to find out about you, do you?"

"Why, Sam? Why?" Stanley asked.

"Because Wendell won't let you stay here," I

said. "He'll tell people about you. Then grown-ups will come and take you away."

"No! No away!" Stanley begged in a frightened voice.

"Well, that's what will happen if Wendell finds you."

I felt bad telling Stanley this. I knew it would scare him. But didn't I *have* to scare him? There was no other way to make him keep out of sight!

Stanley was quiet for a long time. I began to wonder if he was dozing off again. Then he reached up and patted my cheek with a grimy hand.

"Me stay, Sam," he said. "No Wendell. No bad."

"Attaboy," I said. "And I promise it won't be like this forever. Wendell will get tired of working here before long. Then we'll be able to hang out together after school again and do lots of stuff together."

I hoped that was true, anyway.

"I'm getting worried about Stanley," I said to Marjorie in a low voice at lunch the next day. "It's not good for him to be all cooped up like this."

"Maybe he needs a pet," Marjorie answered. "A real pet, not just a turtle. You could get him a—"

Suddenly she stopped talking.

"Get him a what?" I asked.

Then I saw *why* she'd stopped talking. Wendell had been standing right behind us. He walked away quickly when he saw us looking at him.

Had he heard anything? There was no way to tell.

I had promised Stanley that Wendell would get tired of working in the lab. Only he never did. Day after day he shut himself up in the basement. He didn't even bother snooping around the rest of the house anymore.

"How's your work with Dr. Oshrain going, Wendell?" Miss Swang asked one day during science. "You haven't talked about it in a while."

"I am not at liberty to discuss it," Wendell said.

"I see," Miss Swang said. She raised an eyebrow and turned to the blackboard.

Whatever Wendell's new project was, it seemed to have something to do with the cat. At least Creamy always seemed to be down in the lab whenever Wendell was. I could hear her meowing, and sometimes I'd hear Wendell talking to her. But I wasn't curious enough about either Creamy or Wendell to find out what was going on.

One day, though, when Marjorie and I were doing our homework in my room, Wendell came marching up the stairs. He clomped loudly to my doorway and stopped there, waiting for us to turn around.

Marjorie and I pretended not to hear him.

Wendell cleared his throat.

I turned a page in my workbook. Marjorie started to hum a little.

"*Samuel! Marjorie!*" Wendell said sharply.

At last I turned around. "Oh. It's you, Wendell," I said. "What can I do for you?"

"I'd like to invite you and Marjorie down to the lab."

"What for?" Marjorie asked.

Wendell lifted his chin proudly. "To witness an extraordinary scientific event."

Marjorie and I glanced at each other. "No, thanks," we said at the same time.

"You *have* to come. You don't want to miss this." Wendell sounded a little crazed. "Dr. Oshrain's not here, and I need witnesses!"

Marjorie shrugged. "We've got a lot of homework, Wendell," she said. "We're not really interested in—"

"I'm about to clone the cat," Wendell broke in.

"You're *what?*" I blurted out.

"You heard me. I'm about to clone Creamy. I figured out how."

"Sure you did," I answered. "*Sure* you managed to do something *real* scientists can't do!"

"I don't think you realize what a great scientist I really am, Samuel," Wendell said. "I'm *way* more talented than your uncle. I simply reapplied the rules of plant cloning to animal tissue. Some material I found in Dr. Oshrain's notes gave me the idea."

"You mean you went snooping through his desk?" I asked.

"It wasn't snooping. Scientists are allowed to use any information they can, and Dr. Oshrain wasn't in the lab at the time. He was very understanding about it later."

"I bet he was," I said coldly. "Does he know what you're trying to do today?"

"He will—and I'm not just trying, Samuel. I know it's going to work!" Wendell had started dancing up and down. "Come on. It's just about to happen!"

We finally decided to go along with Wendell, just to get him off our backs. "There's no way this is going to work, though," I whispered to Marjorie as we headed down the stairs with Wendell racing ahead.

"Let's try not to laugh too hard when it fails," she whispered back. "At least it's taken his mind off Stanley."

When we got to the lab, I was surprised to see Creamy asleep on the floor. "What's the cat doing down *there*?" I asked, like a dope. I had sort of expected her to be hooked up to a bunch of wires or something. But she was just lying there like the usual slug that she is.

"I don't need the whole cat for the cloning to work," said Wendell. (Kind of a gross way to put it, I thought.) "All I need is a tissue sample." He picked up a glass slide from a counter. "It's right here on this slide."

Now I was even more sure the cloning wouldn't work.

"Perhaps you guests are wondering exactly *how* I will accomplish this cloning," Wendell went on. He sounded like a professor giving a lecture. "Of course I can't give you the full explanation, because you're not intelligent enough to understand it. But I've developed a special amino-acid solution that will activate the cells in Creamy's tissue sample, causing them to generate an entire new creation."

"How did you copy her DNA?" I asked.

Wendell looked surprised that I had even heard of DNA. "Well, I—"

"Oh, don't bother explaining any more, Wendell," Marjorie interrupted. "Just show us how you do it."

"All right, if you're not interested in science," said Wendell angrily. "Here." He picked up an eyedropper, bent over the slide, and carefully dropped one glittering dot of liquid onto it.

For an instant nothing happened.

Then a hissing cloud spouted up off the glass slide. A gray, stinky cloud with little sparks in it. A cloud that grew darker and stinkier by the second.

Horrible fumes—like a mixture of car exhaust and rotten broccoli—filled the lab. The sparks grew bigger and began to dart around like insects. We all began to choke, and I could hear Creamy sneezing on the floor.

"It's not supposed to do this!" Wendell wheezed.

"What are you doing to us, Wendell?" Marjorie shouted in a strangled voice. "Make it stop!"

"I can't stop it!" Wendell squeaked. "I don't know how!"

The hissing grew louder and louder. . . .

The smoke grew darker and thicker. . . .

Then, suddenly, the hissing stopped, and the smoke started to clear. Before any of us could see anything, we heard a new sound.

A hoarse, croaky sound, like the mixture of a cat's meow and a blackboard being scratched by a jagged fingernail.

"MMMMMMMGREOWL!" it went. "MMM-MMMMGREOWL!"

Then came an even *newer* sound.

The sound of a cat burping.

CHAPTER SEVEN

Hi, Cruddy!

Carefully we picked ourselves up off the lab floor. Then we looked over and saw—what?

It was an animal. But was it a cat, exactly?

She was cat*like*, that was for sure. She had ears and a tail and the other things that cats have. But she also had wet, slimy fur that was covered with dustballs. She also had some spots where there was no fur at all—just grayish bald patches. She also had a slug crawling up one foot. She *also* had a nose with greenish slime oozing out of it.

And she smelled. She smelled like five million litter boxes rolled into one.

Creamy took one look and bolted up the stairs, leaving us with Creamy's clone—if that's what she was.

"Well, she's not *exactly* like Creamy," I said.

"It's—it's not my fault!" Wendell cried. "I did the experiment right! I know I did!"

Marjorie patted him on the shoulder. "Maybe it didn't come out perfectly," she said. "Still, you certainly did create another life-form. Whatever it is."

That didn't cheer Wendell up at all. "She's not enough like Creamy!" he said. "She's not *anything* like Creamy! No one would ever believe she was the same cat!"

"Actually, we can see that for ourselves," I said.

"I—I'm a failure!" Wendell said. His chin was trembling. "The world of science will laugh at me!"

"Oh, come on, Wendell," Marjorie said. "No one's going to laugh at you. You did a good job, and—"

"No, I didn't! I'm a failure!" Wendell shrieked. Then he whipped around and glared at me.

"This is all your fault, Samuel!" he howled.

"My fault? What are you talking about?" I asked.

"You must have contaminated my amino-acid solution! You were probably snooping around down here and dropped some of your stupid junk food into it!"

"Wait a sec, Wendell," I said patiently. "I never come down here anymore. And even if I did, I'd know enough not to drop food into an experiment."

"*Sure,*" said Wendell. "You've been out to sabotage me from the very beginning, Samuel. And now you want to humiliate me by making me fail. Well, it won't work!"

He squinted at me. "Do you know what I think?" he asked. "I think that this *thing* on the floor has something to do with that *thing* you called your cousin."

Marjorie and I glanced at each other nervously.

"I'm certain of it, in fact," Wendell went on. "And I'm going to—"

Just then the cat clone walked up to Wendell. Purring, she rubbed her slimy head against his leg. A brownish stain spread across his clean white lab pants.

Then the clone began to bounce. Up and down she went, higher and higher, until at last she bounced right up onto Wendell's shoulder and perched there.

"Don't touch me, you disgusting object!" Wendell shrieked, shaking the cat to the ground. He, too, bolted up the stairs. Then we heard the front door slam overhead.

In the sudden silence the cat gave another hoarse meow. Loudly and raspingly she began to scratch one of her bald patches. A cloud of fleas puffed up into the air.

"Does this cat remind you of anyone?" Marjorie asked.

"A person we know, you mean?" I asked. "A person who lives in a tree?"

The two of us began to laugh.

"What do you think went wrong with the experiment?" Marjorie said.

"I have no idea," I replied. "Stanley's been here in the lab during the days. Probably some of his sweat, or mucus, or toe jam, or earwax—"

"Or spit," Marjorie added.

"Or belly-button lint," I added.

"Or pus," she added.

"Or dandruff," I finished. "Anyway, *some* kind of crud from Stanley's body must have gotten into the amino-acid solution. And the result—"

We glanced over at the result, who was now loudly licking under her tail.

"Stanley would love her, though," said Marjorie. "Hey, let's introduce them!"

I've never seen Stanley as happy as when we woke him up from his nap and brought him to the lab to meet that cat.

"Mess! Pretty!" he bellowed. He squelched over to the new cat (his bare feet left sticky tracks on the floor) and patted her tenderly on the head.

The cat let out a purr that sounded like sandpaper rubbing across glass. Then she bounced up onto Stanley's head and began licking his hair.

"Sam! Sam!" Stanley yelled. "Friend! *Friend!*"

"That's right. You've got a new friend," I said.

"Sam, what name friend?" Stanley asked, tenderly yanking at the cat's foot.

"Ugly," I said promptly. "Let's stick to the truth here."

"It's not the cat's fault she's ugly," Marjorie

objected. "We should give her a nice name to make her feel good about herself. Rose Petal or something."

I tried not to laugh. "Rose Petal is too hard to say," I told her. "Maybe Stanley should get to name her, anyway." I turned to my twin. "What do you want to name the kitty?"

Stanley scratched his head. (Actual drops of grease fell out of his hair onto the floor.) The cat bounced to the ground and rolled under a table. Then she rolled back out and threw up on Stanley's foot.

"Name she Snot!" Stanley suggested excitedly.

"Snot," I repeated, biting my lip. "That's very—uh—"

"No! Doody!" said Stanley. "No! Slug! No! *Cruddy!*"

"I like Cruddy," said Marjorie encouragingly. "And it kind of matches Creamy, too."

"*Cruddy,*" Stanley crooned, putting the cat back on his head. "You good, Cruddy. You mess."

Now the cat leaned down from Stanley's hair to wash his face. Instead of cleaning Stanley's face, though, her tongue left black marks all over it. When she was done, Stanley looked at least fifty percent worse.

"Do you want to keep Cruddy in the tree house with you?" I asked my twin. "I think she'd feel right at home."

Stanley grinned at me. Then he reached up to feel the cat on his head.

"Home, Cruddy," he said. "Come me. Friend."

I went up to visit the two of them that night after supper. As I climbed the ladder, I could hear Stanley's laugh and Cruddy's horrible screeching purr. I peeked through the window and saw that the two of them were playing a game together. It was a simple game. If it had a name, I think it would be called Eat the Flea.

So I pushed the door open a crack and stuck my head in. "Hi, guys," I said.

Both Stanley and Cruddy rushed over to me and stuck out their tongues. "See fleas!" Stanley bragged.

His long, slimy tongue and Cruddy's long, raspy tongue were both speckled with dead fleas.

"Wow," I said. Trying to sound more excited, I added, "Gee. But why aren't you swallowing them?"

"Keeping count," Stanley said. He seemed to be able to talk just as easily with his tongue out as in. "*You* count fleas, Sam. Who am winner?"

"I'll count them later," I said. "But I have to talk to you. Wendell—you remember Wendell?" Stanley nodded and snapped his tongue back into his mouth. "Well, Wendell's pretty upset about Cruddy," I went on. "He made her, you know. I'm worried that he might try to do something."

"Him no take Cruddy!" said Stanley fiercely. He grabbed the cat and pressed her against his chest. Her stomach flattened out like a pancake—another trick she shared with Stanley, I realized.

"I hope he wouldn't want to take Cruddy," I said. "But if you see him around here, let me know."

"Okay, Sam," said my twin cheerfully. He didn't sound too upset. "Look, Cruddy! *Flea!*" he yelled.

He snapped his tongue down to the floor and added another flea to his collection.

The next morning Wendell crawled into our classroom like something that had died in the night. He plodded down the aisle and noisily plunked himself down at his desk.

"Why, Wendell, what's the matter?" Miss Swang asked.

"Nothing's the matter, Miss Swang," Wendell grunted. He put his head down on his desk and closed his eyes.

"Do you want to go to the nurse's office, dear?"

"Uh-uh."

Miss Swang frowned. "Well, then, would you please sit up and join the class?"

"Uh-uh," said Wendell again.

I could tell that Miss Swang was wondering what to do. Finally she said, "Well, if you can follow the lesson that way, I guess it's okay. No, Billy. *You* may not put *your* head down. Everyone else's eyes here, please."

But it was hard for the rest of us to keep our eyes on Miss Swang's arithmetic lesson. Wendell was so much more interesting. He kept groaning and clutching his stomach. Then he would suddenly flail around as if he'd just gotten a shock. None of us could figure out what was going on.

"You don't think he has rabies or something, do you?" I asked Marjorie in the cafeteria at lunchtime. Wendell was lying across the top of a whole table. No one dared to sit near him in case he barfed.

"How could he have rabies?" Marjorie asked. "Cruddy didn't bite him."

"No, but what if there was rabies in her—in her tissue slice, or whatever? What if Wendell caught rabies from that eyedropper?" I couldn't help feeling a little worried about him. "Then I suppose it *would* be sort of my fault. What kind of sandwich did you bring?"

"Tuna. Why would it be your fault?" Marjorie asked.

"Because if I hadn't told Stanley about that stupid garden Wendell planted, Stanley would never have wrecked it. Then Wendell would have kept on working with *plant* cloning, and none of this would have happened. Trade you half my chicken salad for half your tuna."

Mom used to make me pack her horrible left-overs in my lunch bag. Lately, though, she'd started letting me choose my own lunch food. So lunch was my most normal meal nowadays.

Marjorie handed over half her sandwich, and I gave her half of mine. "Now, if you want to make yourself crazy, go ahead," she told me. "Can I have some of your potato chips? Thanks. Anyway, aren't you forgetting that Wendell only started working with your uncle so he could snoop around and find Stanley? It's not as though he's some nice, regular guy who just happened to wander into the lab one day."

"No, I know that. But that doesn't mean I want him to get rabies," I said. "And what if Cruddy is dangerous? We don't know. She might hurt Stanley!"

Marjorie paused. "Probably she wouldn't, though," she said after a second.

I got up to throw my lunch stuff away. "Well, I'm going to talk to Wendell after school. I want to find out more about this experiment. If Cruddy could make people sick, I have to know about it. We could be in danger. And I don't know how much Uncle Zach had to do with the experiment."

"I'll come with you," said Marjorie. "But wait a second. Let me finish your chips first."

On my way to the garbage cans, I stopped by Wendell's table and tapped him on the shoulder.

"Whaddya want?" he mumbled.

"Why are you acting like such a wimp?" I asked.

"Whaddya think?" said Wendell.

"Does that mean you won't be coming to the lab anymore?" I asked. Maybe Stanley would be safe from discovery after all. . . .

"I'm never going back to the lab again," Wendell said. "I'm going home and staying in bed for the rest of my life."

When school let out for the day, Marjorie and I walked over to Wendell's to check on him. (His mother had picked him up as usual. I saw him limp to the car and collapse in the front seat.) I was still a little worried that he might have caught something from Cruddy.

I had never met Mrs. Rice, Wendell's mother, before. When Mrs. Rice answered the doorbell, I was surprised to see how normal she was. Just like a regular mom in exercise clothes and sneakers—not at all like a Wendell-type mom.

"Hi, guys," she said. "What can I do for you?"

We introduced ourselves, and I explained, "We came by to see if Wendell was feeling any better."

"Why, isn't that nice of you!" exclaimed Mrs. Rice. "I've been wishing Wendell had some real friends!"

Marjorie and I both looked away. We wouldn't

have dreamed of telling such a nice woman that we were just there to check Wendell for symptoms. It must be awful for parents when their kids are unpopular. Unless they're the kind of parents I have, who never notice that kind of thing.

"To tell you the truth, I'm worried about Wendell," Mrs. Rice went on. "He's been acting odd for the last day or so. Odd even for Wendell."

Marjorie and I glanced at each other in surprise. Mothers aren't usually so honest about their children.

"Go on up and see if you can make him feel better," Mrs. Rice urged us. "I'm sure he'd love to see you."

She turned out to be wrong about that.

Marjorie and I found Wendell lying facedown on his bed. He was moaning something I couldn't make out into his pillow.

"What's that you're saying, Wendell?" I asked.

"Failure!" Wendell moaned. "I'm a failure!"

"That's all you're worried about?" I asked, amazed.

"What else is there?" Wendell asked dramatically.

"You mean you're really not sick?" I blurted out.

At that, Wendell rolled over to face us. "*Sick?* What are you talking about?" he asked in his regular voice.

"I—I thought maybe that cat you cloned had

given you some kind of sickness." I was starting to feel a little stupid.

"Don't talk about that cat!" Wendell screeched. "Do you have to rub it in? Are you *trying* to embarrass me?"

"No!" I said. "I'm trying to be nice to you!"

"Trying to be nice by humiliating me. *I* see," said Wendell crossly.

"Anyway, the cat's not so bad," Marjorie said. "She's—she's even kind of cute."

"She is *not* cute," Wendell argued. "She's a disgusting mutant."

"That's why she's so perfect for Stanley, though," I said. "I mean, they're both kind of disgusting, and they're having a great time together up in his tree house. The cat sleeps on Stanley's bed at night, and—"

Suddenly I stopped, feeling sick to my stomach. Wendell was sitting up on his bed now. His expression had totally changed.

"I thought you said Stanley was your cousin," he said.

"I—I did," I faltered.

"I thought you said he was going back to Tree."

"I did. I mean, he did. Go back, I mean."

Wendell cocked his head to one side. "But you say he and that cat are playing in the tree *house*?"

"No, I—I didn't say that," I stammered.

"Yes, you did," said Wendell slowly. He swung his legs off the bed. All of a sudden he looked much healthier.

"I have to thank you, Samuel," he said, "for reminding me of why I first went to work for your uncle. I got a little sidetracked when I was working on my clone, but now I can return to my original mission."

I was opening and closing my mouth like a guppy. "But I—but I—"

"You can go now," Wendell interrupted. "See you at school. Don't forget to do your homework."

"Wendell, what are you talking about?" asked Marjorie.

"Ask Samuel," Wendell told her.

"What *is* Wendell talking about?" Marjorie repeated nervously when we got outside.

"He's talking about how I just blew it. He's saying that now he *knows* Stanley isn't my cousin. He's thinking that Stanley is a clone, just the way he thought. Just the way I *thought* he thought."

"And what does he mean about getting sidetracked, and about his original mission and everything?"

I sighed. Everything I had been afraid of was happening. "His original mission—when he got the job with Uncle Zach—was to find out about Stanley and expose him to the world. He got sidetracked when he started working on his own clone. Now he's realizing that even though the experiment with Cruddy didn't work out, there's another way he can become famous. All he has to do is prove to everyone that there really *is* a Stanley. Then Wendell will get all the attention he wants. And poor Stanley will end up in some kind of zoo—or worse!"

CHAPTER EIGHT

Moonlight Madness

"I really wrecked things, didn't I?" I said sadly as Marjorie and I walked home. "I should never have worried about Wendell. I should have realized that Cruddy couldn't have rabies if Creamy was healthy. I should never have jumped to conclusions. I should have gone home and done my homework and eaten supper and gone to bed like a good boy."

We had reached Marjorie's house, and she turned to me. "What do you want me to say, Sam?" she asked. "I agree with you." She tossed her head and headed up her front walk.

Okay. So Marjorie wasn't going to help me protect Stanley from Wendell. Well, I'd just have to do it myself. I went up to my room and started drawing up a plan. . . .

"Did Wendell come over today?" my mother asked at supper that night (squash with peanuts, and baked guavas).

I shook my head.

"I thought not," said Mom. "Creamy is behaving very strangely. I think she's started to depend on Wendell and his visits."

It was true that Creamy wasn't acting like her usual self. What I mean is, she wasn't lying in a fat heap on the floor. Instead, she was pacing back and forth, meowing anxiously, and staring at the back door.

"Is there something out there, Creamy?" Mom finally asked her. She got up and opened the door for the cat. Creamy just shivered and backed away.

"Well, I hope Wendell will be back tomorrow," said my mother. "I guess Creamy misses him."

I could have told Mom it wasn't that. Creamy knew, in her cat way, that Cruddy was out in the tree house with Stanley. Cats can never make up their minds, and it seemed that Creamy didn't know whether she wanted to see Cruddy or not. After all, Cruddy was her own flesh and blood—sort of.

I couldn't settle down that night, either. I was sure Wendell was going to come snooping around looking for the tree house. I had to be ready when he got there!

As soon as Mom and Dad had gone to bed, I tiptoed out of my room and outdoors.

There was no moon that night, and for a second I wasn't even sure if I was going in the right direction. Then I caught the welcome scent of five million litter boxes rolled into one, and realized that I must be heading toward Cruddy and the tree house.

The horrible grinding sound I heard had to be Stanley and Cruddy snoring. Stanley was the one who sounded like a chain saw. That meant Cruddy must be the one who sounded like pebbles in a garbage disposal.

I stretched out my hands to make sure I wouldn't bang into Stanley's tree. After fumbling around for a few seconds, I bumped into the rope ladder and climbed up.

Stanley's tree house had one of those rechargeable glow-in-the-dark night-lights. (I recharged it for him in the house.) In the dim, greenish light I could see my twin hunched up in his bed. Cruddy was sitting on Stanley's head. Both of them were snoring, and both of them were blowing big spit-bubbles as they snored. It would be hard to say which of them had worse night breath. I guess it depends on whether you prefer breath that smells like stale barf (Stanley's) or breath that smells like rotten fish (Cruddy's).

"Stanley!" I hissed, shaking his shoulder. "Wake up!"

"Get out of here," Stanley said clearly. He rolled over onto his stomach and stayed asleep. (That was the only time I've ever heard him say a complete sentence.)

I tried to wake Cruddy, too. I even tried jabbing her claws into Stanley's arm in the hopes that *one* of them would wake up. But Cruddy just flopped around like a stuffed toy. I guess she had also "inherited" Stanley's sleeping habits.

Well, maybe that would make it easier to booby-trap the tree house. The two of them wouldn't get in my way.

I glanced around the tree house. Stanley's craft supplies were what I was looking for. In a second I saw them piled messily in one corner. I pulled out the play dough first. It was filled with twigs and dust, but that wouldn't matter. It was still pretty wet and mushy—I guessed that Stanley had been drooling into it. I tucked a big blob of it under my arm and climbed quietly back down the ladder again.

I spread the blob of play dough in a big messy smear at the bottom of the ladder. If Wendell stepped in it, I knew he'd have to stop to scrape it off his shoes. That would delay him long enough for me to put the bats into action.

The bats? Yes, the bats. Working quickly, I folded some out of construction paper. I wanted bats to swoop down onto Wendell as he started climbing the ladder. What could I tie them to? I wondered. Stanley didn't have any string. I finally decided to throw them down at Wendell like paper airplanes. That would probably look more realistic anyway.

Now, the ladder itself. There was a bottle of glue somewhere in the pile of craft supplies, I knew. We had used it the day we showed Stanley how to make a piñata. (My twin hadn't quite gotten the idea. He had put the piñata over his head. "Hit me!" he had shouted happily.) I rummaged around until I found the glue. Then I painted the rope ladder with a thick, sticky layer. The glue stuck to the rope very nicely.

Last of all, I rigged a bottle of honey over the tree house door. Stanley could always be counted on to have some kind of sticky food in his tree house.

Smiling to myself, I settled down to wait.

It wasn't exactly restful sitting in the tree house with all that snoring. But I actually managed to doze a little until the sharp beam of a high-intensity flashlight bobbed into my eyes and woke me.

Quickly I sat up and listened. Yes, someone was coming through the yard toward the tree house. And to judge by the crashing I heard, it was someone who didn't know much about walking through the woods.

The crashing came nearer.

Then someone banged into the foot of the tree.

I moved quietly over to the window. I couldn't see much because the flashlight was so bright. But the shrill, prissy voice I heard was definitely Wendell's.

He was hissing to himself, "Don't give up. Remember your mission. Scientific advancement.

Kidnap clone. Bring clone to school. Embarrass Samuel. *Destroy* Samuel. Oh, dear! How vile! What *is* this stuff?"

He had just stepped in the blob of play dough.

"Dog mess!" Wendell wailed in a loud whisper. He started frantically scraping his foot on the grass. "Hideous! Germy!"

After about ten minutes of scraping, he grabbed the ladder and stepped onto the first rung.

He got stuck instantly. It was very good glue.

While Wendell was trying to wrestle his feet off the ladder, I leaned out the window and launched the horde of paper bats toward his head. *Zing! Zing! Zing!* As the bats zoomed past Wendell, he let out a high, terrified scream. What a baby! He was so scared that he tumbled backward off the ladder. It was lucky he'd only gotten stuck on the *first* rung, because his feet stayed glued to the ladder as he fell. It was also lucky— from a not-getting-hurt point of view—that his head landed on that blob of play dough.

"Dog mess in my *hair*!" I heard Wendell moan to himself.

He didn't try to clean his hair off. I guess he figured it was useless. Instead he wrenched his feet loose and began climbing the ladder again, rung by sticky rung. Each rung held him back for about three minutes, I figured—he was really struggling. At last, panting and wheezing, he made it to the top.

Just as Wendell's hand touched the tree house deck, I jerked the string tied to the honey jar over the door.

A wave of honey slurped out of the jar in a perfect arc. Perfect, I mean, because it hit Wendell right in the face. He slid down the ladder and landed on the ground again. That's when I poked my head out of the tree house window.

"Hi, dog mess," I said calmly. "I mean, Wendell."

"S-Samuel!" he exclaimed. "What are you doing here?"

"I could ask you the same thing," I said. (Behind me, the horrible snoring held steady.) "In fact, I think I *will* ask you the same thing. What are you doing here?"

"Just taking a stroll," Wendell answered as he picked himself up off the ground and aimed his flashlight at me.

"Aim that thing away from me," I ordered. "Why are you taking a stroll on my property in the middle of the night?"

"It's not *your* property," Wendell answered loftily. "It belongs to your parents. You're not smart enough to earn a living. I have a perfect right to—"

"WHAZZAT?" Stanley suddenly shouted. He bounced out of bed so hard that he hit the ceiling.

Maybe that's what woke up Cruddy.

"MMMMMMGREEEEOOOOOOOOOOOOWW-WWWWWLLLLLL!" she shrieked.

Then what looked like a yowling bolt of lightning—dirty, ratty lightning—flew out the tree house door and landed smack on top of Wendell's head.

It was Cruddy, of course. I guess she was defending her territory against an alien intruder. (I wonder if she knew the intruder was also her creator.)

For the second time that night, Wendell tumbled backward onto the mess—this time because Cruddy's claws were digging into his head. Wendell sat up and grabbed at her, but Cruddy wouldn't budge. She had caught her prey, and she wasn't about to let go.

Yowling almost as loudly as Cruddy, Wendell stumbled to his feet. "All right!" he said grimly. "I'll take *you* to school instead!"

Cruddy was still holding on as Wendell lurched out of the yard.

"Whazzat?" Stanley called again. "Cruddy! Where?"

"Wendell has her!" I said over my shoulder. "Come on! We've got to catch them!"

Stanley was at my side in an instant. "We *go!*" he shouted.

"We *shhhhhhhh!*" I hissed. "Don't make so much noise! We don't want to wake up Mom and Dad!"

That was all it took. Stanley vaulted off the tree house platform into the dark. He hit the ground as silently as a cat (a cat not riding on

Wendell's head, I mean). Then he whispered impatiently up to me.

"Sam! You come?"

"Hold on!" I said, frantically rummaging through a moldy pile of clothes to find Stanley some pants.

Stanley couldn't wait. He bounced up, grabbed me, and bounced back down to the ground again. The two of us went up and down for a few bounces before we landed. Then Stanley pulled on the pants and jerked me to my feet. For once I could tell that *I* was driving *him* crazy. "Go! Come! Hurrying!" he muttered.

"I can't go as fast as you, Stanley!" I whispered back. "You can see in the dark better than I can!"

So Stanley started dragging me through the yard.

We bumped along over the lumpy grass until we reached the sidewalk. My feet were barely touching the ground.

"Let me walk now, Stanley!" I whispered.

He wouldn't slow down.

In the streetlights I could see Wendell zigzagging a block ahead of us. He was heading toward our school—and Cruddy was still riding his head like a surfer.

Wendell led us down one block, then another. Stanley can run unbelievably fast, but I guess I slowed him down. (Also, he stopped a couple of times to investigate some interesting-looking gar-

bage cans at the curb.) And I guess Cruddy speeded Wendell up. We narrowed the gap, but we couldn't quite catch up to Wendell.

Then Wendell turned right, and left again, and left again, and then right—and then I lost count. Suddenly Stanley stopped dead. *And* dropped me on the sidewalk.

"Where he?" he muttered.

Rubbing my smarting knees, I got slowly to my feet and looked around. We'd reached my school. But where was Wendell? The school yard was lit by the parking lot lights. The school halls were lit up as well. But there was no trace of Wendell inside or out.

For a moment Stanley and I stared at each other in dismay. Then, from somewhere, I thought I heard a hoarse, grating, squealing sound—like nails on a blackboard or metal being sawed in half. It almost sounded like—

"Cruddy!" Stanley yelled gleefully.

He pointed toward the west wing of the school. "There!"

He cocked his head to one side and listened again.

"Wendell," he muttered, sniffing the air. "Wendell. Cruddy."

"Wendell is with Cruddy?" I asked, and Stanley nodded. "Well, then, lead the way," I told him.

Eagerly my twin yanked me toward the west wing. But when we got to the front door, we stopped in dismay. It was bolted shut.

"Wendell probably has his own key—that goody-goody," I said. I could just see him convincing the principal that he needed one so he could do extra studying. "Now what are we— Wait, Stanley! *You* can get in!"

As I've told you already, one of Stanley's special skills is being able to flatten himself paper-thin so he can slither under doors. I've seen him do it lots of times, but I never get used to how weird it looks.

"You slide on in and unbolt the door," I told him.

Stanley nodded. Before I could blink, he had slithered under the door and disappeared. There was a scrabbling sound from inside. Then Stanley pushed the door open for me. (I wondered what the school custodian would say when he saw the slime there.)

"I'll look down this way," I whispered, pointing to the right. "You go in that direction." I pointed Stanley left. "Call me if you need help."

With one *boing!* Stanley had bounced to the end of the corridor. Then he bounced around the corner and disappeared.

I had been searching the empty, echoing halls for about five minutes when I heard a thud.

Then came another thud. Then a cat's yowl. And the sound of a heavy metal door being slammed.

From behind me, I heard sneaky footsteps padding down the corridor.

Stanley, I knew, had never taken a sneaky step in his life. So I darted behind the drinking fountain and peeked out—just in time to see Wendell tiptoeing toward the front door of the building, muttering to himself. There was no cat on his head this time.

As Wendell was pushing open the heavy front door, I heard the tiny, metallic *ping!* of something hitting the floor. The instant the door swung shut, I dashed up to see what he'd dropped.

There, lying on the school's industrial-size doormat, was a key. Was it Wendell's? Or had he just kicked it while he was leaving?

Well, I decided to hang on to the key until I knew. If it *was* Wendell's, I'd be able to cause him a little trouble by keeping it. I slipped the key into my pocket, then watched out the front door as Wendell raced clumsily across the school yard and disappeared into the shadows.

A minute later Stanley ran up to meet me on the landing. Cruddy was tucked safely inside his shirt, her scraggly head peeking out under his chin.

"Where were you? Where'd you find Cruddy?" I asked.

Stanley drew a deep breath. "Wendell me lock door lock Cruddy fight lock door room lock fight!" he burst out.

Okay, at least I got the part about the lock. "Wendell locked Cruddy up somewhere?" I asked.

Stanley nodded. "Me, too," he said.

"And he locked you up when you came after Cruddy?"

"Yuh."

"And you slid out under the door with Cruddy?"

He nodded.

"So the door is still locked," I said slowly. I was sure the key in my pocket would open it.

Again he nodded. "Show?" he asked.

"Yes, I want you to show me. Where is this room?"

As Stanley dragged me back down the hall, Cruddy began to yowl. "Okay," Stanley soothed her. "Now okay. Wendell am poophead," he crooned. "He no nice."

When we reached the end of the hall, Stanley pointed toward a tiny room filled with art supplies. There was just space for one person—holding one cat.

"So this is where Wendell locked you up," I said. "Did he say anything?"

My twin's face screwed up with the effort of trying to explain. "Say lock stay show teacher stay morning trap clone," he told me rapidly.

"Wait a sec. I think I'm getting better at translating this. Wendell said you would stay locked up there until morning, and then he would show you to Miss Swang?"

"Yuh. Class."

"And her class—*my* class," I said.

"Yuh. Sam, what am clone?"

"A clone is a special kind of twin," I said carefully. "Clones are made, not born—so that makes them extra interesting. You're *my* clone. And Cruddy is Creamy's."

"Clone am good?"

"Yes. Very good," I said absently. I was already thinking about my next problem.

What was the best way to get revenge on Wendell now?

He had kidnapped Cruddy and tried to imprison my clone. I couldn't let him get away with it.

What would drive Wendell crazier than anything else?

Well, I had seen how fast Wendell had fallen apart when he had created Cruddy instead of cloning Creamy. He couldn't bear to make mistakes, it seemed. So what would it be like for him if the whole class—and his teacher— watched him make a really, really big mistake?

I thought about that, and then I started to smile.

CHAPTER NINE

Wendell Takes a Fall

"You no stay!" Stanley wailed when I explained my plan to him. "Home me!"

"I *will* come home after school," I promised. "But for now, I'm going to rest right in this little room here." (*Little* was right. I hoped I wouldn't lean up against the paper cutter by mistake.) "You can lock me in"—I handed him the key—"and take Cruddy home with you," I went on.

Stanley sniffed the key curiously. His face squinched up with disgust. "Wendell!" he groaned. "Me flush toilet!"

"No, no, don't do that," I said hastily. "We need this key. Just put it into Wendell's locker, okay? You can slide it through the vent at the top."

"What am locker?" asked my twin.

I pointed around us. "*These* are lockers. Kids keep their stuff in them. Wendell will think he just dropped the key into his locker by mistake."

"Sam, where am Wendell locker?" was Stanley's next question.

I paused. I wasn't sure myself. "You can find it, Stanley!" I finally said, with more confidence than I felt. "All you have to do is walk up and down the halls sniffing the locker-door handles. You'll be able to tell which one is Wendell's, won't you?"

Stanley frowned. "Yuh. But me hate. Bad job. You come home me!"

"I really can't," I told him firmly. "I need your help, though, Stanley."

I grabbed a piece of paper from one of the shelves and pulled a pencil out of my pocket. Then I scribbled Mom and Dad a quick note saying that I had left for school before they had woken up. "I'm working on a special project," I finished the note. (At least it was the truth.)

"Can you just put this note under the front door of the house when you get home?" I asked Stanley.

He shook his head, his chin quivering.

"Oh, go ahead," I urged him. "I'll be fine in here. I'll sleep, and I'll do some projects with these supplies. Just the way you've been doing in your tree house."

Stanley still looked worried, but at last he agreed to go along with my plan—after I did one thing for him.

"Kiss Cruddy g'bye," he urged me. "Love!" Before I could argue, Stanley had pressed Cruddy's sticky face up against my lips.

Yuck! First I got a mouthful of dirt-crusted fur. Then Cruddy's nose smeared against my tongue—it was like licking a slug. Then *her* raspy tongue scraped against *my* nose like a burr. (Of course that spread Cruddy's bad breath to exactly the place I could smell it most easily.) Finally, for good measure, she dug her claws into my shoulders. I spent the rest of the night picking bits of fur and dirt off my face.

Not that there was much *left* of the night. By the time Stanley finally locked me into the art-supply room, it was almost dawn. Through a little vent in the wall I could hear the first birds starting to chirp. I knew I still had a long wait before school started, so I settled down on the floor and started thinking.

Now that I was cooped up myself, I felt terrible about making Stanley stay in his tree house all this time. If I hated it—and I knew I was going to get out soon—I could just imagine how Stanley must feel. *Like a buffalo in a matchbox*, I thought. I promised that as soon as I could, I'd figure out a better setup for Stanley.

I tried to make myself comfortable, but it wasn't easy. Bare linoleum isn't much fun to sit on, and a stack of construction paper doesn't make a very good pillow. But I didn't care. The important thing was that in the morning I would spoil Wendell's plan and save Stanley.

Once everyone had arrived at school, Wendell

was planing to unlock the supply closet and reveal Stanley to the world. But it wasn't going to work.

I smiled happily as I pillowed my head on the construction paper. I couldn't wait to see Wendell's face when he unlocked the door.

The first bell jarred me to my feet, trembling. The house is on fire! I thought. Then I remembered where I was.

I hadn't expected to fall asleep, but obviously I had dozed off. My eyes felt sandy, my hair felt oily, and my teeth felt as though they had been rubbed with wax. I could easily have passed for Stanley. I was hoping I didn't have much longer to wait.

Kids were starting to trickle into the building. I listened to scraps of their conversations as they went by.

". . . with mustard," I heard a girl say firmly. "You have to do it with mustard, or the curl won't set right."

". . . won't let me go to the concert," a boy complained. "It's so unfair! Patty got to go to concerts when *she* was twelve."

"Bananas have lots of . . ."

"So I told her where she could put her . . ."

". . . but I'm going to see if I can get her to raise it to an A plus. I'm too good a student to have just an A on my record."

I sat up alertly. That was Wendell. He was here.

I could hear him opening his locker, which turned out to be right near the art-supply room. (I hoped Stanley had managed to find it.) He was muttering to himself.

"Let's see," he said. "Dental floss . . . yes. Math book . . . yes. Daily study record . . . yes. Oh, here's my key! I wondered where that was." (I breathed a big sigh of relief.) "All right," Wendell finished. "I think that's everything."

A second after that I heard his voice, low, outside my door. "Are you still in there?" he asked.

I didn't answer.

"Hey!" Wendell said sharply. "Make some noise."

I kicked the door as hard as I could.

"Not *that* much noise!" Wendell snapped. "Do you want people to find out you're in there? I mean . . ." He stopped, realizing that I probably *did* want people to find out I was in there. "Oh, never mind," he said with an exasperated sigh. "Just be a good little clone for now."

The second bell rang then, and I heard Wendell marching off to class. Half an hour must have passed before I heard voices in the hall again.

One of them was Miss Swang's. She didn't sound very pleased to be out in the hall.

"I don't see how this story can be true, Wendell. And I don't appreciate your making us hike through the halls this way. I know we're doing science reports, but I didn't expect you to throw in a gym class, too."

"But it's such an amazing event, Miss Swang," Wendell said earnestly. "You see, while I was perfecting my cloning experiments, I made an astonishing discovery. Dr. Oshrain has already created a human clone—a clone of Samuel Moore. And I have the clone right here in school!"

"Why doesn't Sam's uncle have the clone of Sam, if he's the one who invented it?" asked Elayne Munter.

Wendell's voice was dark. "Because when I left Dr. Oshrain's lab yesterday, the clone followed me and attacked me."

I held back an angry gasp.

"I—I had to come back to school to pick up something from my locker, and the clone ambushed me on my way out of the building. I think it must have been lying in wait for human prey.

"I fought it for more than an hour before I was able to subdue it," Wendell continued solemnly. "It's a brute. It looks identical to Samuel, but it has a terrible, fiendish strength. It can't even speak English properly—it just bellows and mumbles."

Bellows and mumbles *both*? I wanted to say.

"Maybe you'd better not let it out of the supply room," suggested Elayne Munter nervously. "Why don't you just call the police and have them take it away?"

"Because I was able to subdue it," Wendell repeated. "I don't think it will bother us anymore."

"How did you get the key to the art-supply room anyway, Wendell?" asked Miss Swang. "And how did you get into the school?"

Wendell paused. "I—I'll explain that once I've made my presentation," he said quickly. I could tell he was hoping that Miss Swang would forget about it in her amazement at seeing Stanley.

"That clone sure is being quiet," Chris Burbank said cheerfully. "I hope it didn't *die* in there."

"Clones can't die," Wendell informed him.

This, I was sure, was totally wrong. A clone is supposed to be an exact copy of another living thing. I bet a clone can die just the way any other living thing can.

Wendell's words gave me an idea, though. As he turned the key in the lock, I lay down on the floor and tried to look dead.

When Wendell opened the door, and the class crowded around him to see into the supply room, what they saw was me lying there with my eyes closed.

"Oh, no," Wendell muttered. "Maybe there wasn't enough air in here!"

"You've killed it!" said Elayne shrilly. "You've killed the clone, Wendell!"

"N-no, I haven't!" Wendell stammered. "I couldn't have! I—I—"

At that moment I let out a huge yawn. I

stretched, opened my eyes, and bounced to my feet. "Hi, Wendell," I said cheerfully. "Boy, what a great night's sleep I had. Are you done with your game now?"

Wendell stepped back, pale and sick looking. I almost felt sorry for him. (But not quite.)

"Just a minute," said Chris Burbank. "That's no clone of Sam. That *is* Sam!"

Wendell was still goggling. "No, it's—it's—"

"Of course it's me," I said robustly. "Is it time for school yet? Wendell agreed to let me out when school started."

"I did not!" said Wendell indignantly.

"What? You mean you were going to make Sam *stay* in here?" gasped Elayne Munter. "Wendell, that's so mean!"

"No, I wasn't going to—" Wendell spluttered. "I mean, I was—it was—"

Now Miss Swang stepped forward and took charge. "Just a minute," she said sternly. "Wendell, we've already heard *your* version of the story. Now I'd like to hear Sam's side. That *is* you, Sam, isn't it?" she added with a touch of sarcasm. "You're not a clone of yourself, I trust?"

"Of course not," I said, grinning. "I'm just Sam."

"No, you're not!" Wendell insisted. "You're just a *clone*! Look what a mess he is!" he appealed to the class.

I sighed—very artistically, I thought. "Well,

you wouldn't look that great if someone had locked *you* up in here all night." Then I turned back to Miss Swang. "I don't know why, but Wendell got kind of mad at me yesterday. He was working in my uncle's lab, and he wrecked up one of the experiments. Uncle Zachary was really nice about it, but the next thing I knew, Wendell was having a total fit. When Uncle Zach was out of the room, Wendell snuck up behind me and knocked me over the head with a Bunsen burner. Pretty sneaky, Wendell," I added.

But Miss Swang was frowning at *me* now. "A Bunsen burner? Sam, you're showing more imagination than you've ever shown in your written work," she said disapprovingly. "Are you sure this is all true?"

"Well, maybe it wasn't a Bunsen burner," I said quickly. "Maybe I just fell and hurt my head—yes, I guess that's it. Then I guess Wendell must have dragged me here while I was unconscious."

"Dragged you here?" asked Chris Burbank. "*Wendell* could drag someone all that way?"

"I think he was desperate," I answered. "So desperate that he turned extra-strong. Also, I seem to remember him resting a lot." This story was going to get away from me if I wasn't careful.

"Why did Wendell want you here in school?" asked Miss Swang with another frown.

I paused. I hadn't thought of that, either. I decided it probably sounded more Wendell-ish to freak out from overwork than to go crazy and start acting like a monster.

"I think maybe Wendell really thought I *was* a clone at that point," I said. "He wanted to create a clone really badly, you know. I think he just worked so hard that he started seeing double. And once he thought I was a clone, he couldn't wait to show me off to everybody.

"When I woke up," I went on, "I heard Wendell saying something about how I was a menace. We were both in the hall outside this supply room. And Wendell was unlocking it."

"Where did he get the key?" asked Miss Swang.

"I don't know," I said truthfully enough. "I think maybe he—cloned it?"

"I did *not!*" Wendell gasped. He was getting pale. "I made this key with my skeleton-key kit!"

"Why, Wendell," said Miss Swang, "that's very dishonest."

"I'm the one who's being honest!" Wendell shouted. "Everything this *clone* is telling you is a lie!"

"So then Wendell got down on his knees and *begged* me to stay in the closet until he could show me to everyone," I went on. "He said it was the only way he could prove how smart he was." (I was starting to enjoy this!)

"What?" Wendell bit out the words. "You know none of that is true! I locked you and that clone cat in here fair and square!"

I sighed patiently. "Wendell, I only said you could lock me in because I felt sorry for you. I didn't want to be mean when you'd been working so hard. And my head was still sore from my fall, so I didn't really mind the thought of lying down for a little while. Anyway, *what* cat? If there were a cat in here, I think I'd know about it."

Now Wendell looked as though he were about to pull his own head off. "I—what—she must have—this—you—I—You *are* a clone! I can prove it!" he screamed. "What are the steps taken in synthesizing glycoproteins? What's the square root of ninety-four? Answer me!"

I stared at him, genuinely confused. "Wendell, what are you talking about? I don't know!"

"You see? That *proves* it!" Wendell shrieked at Miss Swang. "He doesn't know anything! He can't answer the simplest questions! Because he's a clone!"

"Wendell, you're not making sense," said Miss Swang. "You haven't proved anything. No ordinary fifth-grader knows how to synthesize glycoproteins. Even *I* don't know."

"Maybe you're a clone, too," I suggested jokingly.

Wendell whirled around to face me. From his angry expression, I could tell that he was finally starting to suspect I might actually be Sam after all. "You dolt!" he howled. "You clod! You oaf! You ignoramus! You—"

"That's enough from you, Wendell." Miss Swang's voice was angrier than I had ever heard it. "I want you to go right down to the principal's office and wait for me until I can sort out what's going on here."

Then her voice softened. "Sam, you must be very tired. Why don't you go to the nurse's office and rest awhile?"

It was the best idea anyone could have had. Construction paper makes a terrible pillow.

As I headed down the hall to the nurse's office, I suddenly stopped and sniffed. What was that awful smell? It was like a landfill! But there weren't any landfills around here, and—

Then I saw Stanley slithering through one of the hall windows. First his paper-flat feet came through, and then the rest of him. When he landed on the floor and turned three-dimensional again, I raced over to him.

"What are you doing here, Stanley?" I whispered, glancing quickly back over my shoulder to make sure no one else was in the hall. "You're supposed to be at home! You can't keep showing up at school like this!"

"Me help you!" Stanley whimpered. "Get bad Wendell!"

"I don't need any help!" I said. "I'm just on

my way down to the—"

Then I froze. I could hear footsteps rounding the corner toward us. *Adult* footsteps—I could tell from the clacking of the shoe leather.

"Someone's coming!" I whispered. "We've got to—"

"Me help," Stanley broke in confidently. "You rest."

He yanked open the nearest locker door and shoved me inside. Before I could even find the door handle, he was walking down the hall.

"Hello, Sam," I heard a woman say. It was Mrs. Murtag, the school nurse! "Goodness, you look—uh—rumpled! Miss Swang called and asked me to keep an eye out for you," she went on. "She was worried that you might need some help."

"No worry," I heard Stanley say. "Me am Sam, not Stanley. It am okay."

Inside the locker, I buried my face in my hands.

Mrs. Murtag didn't answer right away. And when she did, she sounded worried. "You really *do* need a rest, don't you, Sam?" she asked. "Let's get you right down to my office so you can lie down."

"Lie down," Stanley echoed. "Pick nose."

"Uh—right," said Mrs. Murtag after a second.

As soon as the sound of their footsteps had disappeared around the corner, I pushed the locker door open and peeked out into the hall. Then I ran quietly down the hall after my twin and Mrs. Murtag.

Let's see, I thought as I tiptoed along. All I have to do is station myself somewhere near the nurse's office and hide. Then, when Mrs. Murtag goes out of the office for something, I can sneak in and change places with Stanley. And all I'll have to do after that is explain why I sound so different and why I'm wearing different clothes from the ones Mrs. Murtag just saw on Stanley. That shouldn't be hard.

Or, rather, I knew it would be hard—incredibly hard—but I didn't have a choice, did I?

Hair Balls and Happy Endings

"So no one caught you?" asked Marjorie that afternoon. She, Stanley, and I were sitting up in the tree house sharing a quart of chocolate-chip ice cream. (Stanley had crushed some pinecones onto his share.)

"Of course not," I said airily. "I waited in the janitor's closet next to the nurse's office. It wasn't locked, luckily—Boy, I've sure had enough of sitting around in little tiny spaces. When I heard Mrs. Murtag leave her office, I went in and traded places with Stanley. I pretended to be sleeping when she came back in. When I pretended to wake up, Mrs. Murtag just said how much better I looked after my rest. Stanley and I were both such a mess, though, that I don't think she even noticed our clothes were different."

"And Miss Swang believed you okay?"

"Oh, yeah. Enough, anyway. No one except Wendell would believe that someone like Stanley actually exists." I smiled at my twin. "Wendell's in a lot of trouble, by the way. Miss Swang got really mad at him for locking me in the closet. It could have been very dangerous if there was a fire, she told him. So now Wendell is going to return his key to the school, and turn in his skeleton-key kit—I wonder where he got it, by the way. It would be useful to have—and write an essay about getting along with others. Which may take him forever to finish. I don't think he has a clue about how to get along with others."

"He no here today," added Stanley with satisfaction, shaking a little dandruff into his ice cream.

"That's right. Uncle Zachary fired him when Stanley told him about Wendell kidnapping Cruddy," I told Marjorie. "And he said he'd take care of Stanley while we're at school, so Stanley won't get bored when he's awake."

"Let's just hope no one ever makes a clone of *Wendell*," Marjorie said with a chuckle.

I smiled at my twin. "We'll be able to play in the lab and the woods again after school, Stanley. You won't have to stay all by yourself in the tree house."

"Teach me read more, Sam?"

"Sure, we'll keep working on that. How are you doing with your reading, by the way?" I asked.

"Me spell, Sam!" Stanley said excitedly. "Listen. Burp am B-U-P."

Marjorie and I stared at him in amazement. "That's pretty good!" I said. "We'll have you reading in no time."

"Cruddy read, too?" asked Stanley eagerly.

I laughed. "Well, we'll do our best with Cruddy. She's been a really good friend to you, hasn't she?"

Stanley nodded and lovingly drooled a little ice cream onto Cruddy's head.

I could have sworn there was a smile on Cruddy's patchy, balding face. "You're right," she seemed to be saying to me. "Stanley and I make a great team, don't we?"

Then she leaned over and coughed an enormous hair ball into my lap.

"Yuck!" I jumped to my feet. The hair ball splatted to the ground. My twin picked it up and eyed it with interest.

"What *this*?" he asked.

"That's a hair ball," I said with disgust. "Hair balls are one of the things you have to get used to with cats, Stanley. Especially with a cat who has long fur, like Cruddy. Where she has fur, that is," I added. "Anyway, cats wash themselves so much that sometimes they swallow some fur, and—"

"NO, STANLEY!" Marjorie suddenly shrieked. "Don't you *dare!*"

But it was too late. The sodden mass of cat hair was already halfway down Stanley's throat.

My twin gave an enormous gulp. And an equally enormous burp. Then he turned to us with a happy smile.

"Just like Cruddy," he said proudly. "Cruddy my friend. F-R-E-N. Friend."

ANN HODGMAN is a former children's book editor and the author of over twenty-five children's books, including the popular *My Babysitter Is a Vampire*, *My Babysitter Has Fangs*, *My Babysitter Bites Again*, and *Stinky Stanley*. In addition to humorous fiction for children, she has written teen mysteries and non-fiction for reluctant readers. She lives with her husband and two children in Washington, Connecticut.

JOHN EMIL CYMERMAN was born in Philadelphia and studied there at the Hussian School of Art, where he now teaches. He lives in Pitman, New Jersey with his wife and children.